LUCIFER'S DAUGHTER

Borgo Press Books by VICTOR J. BANIS

*The Astral: Till the Day I Die * Avalon: An Historical Novel * The C.A.M.P. Cookbook * The C.A.M.P. Guide to Astrology * Charms, Spells, and Curses for the Millions * Color Him Gay: That Man from C.A.M.P. * The Curse of Bloodstone: A Gothic Novel of Terror * Darkwater: A Gothic Novel of Horror * The Daughters of Nightsong: An Historical Novel* (Nightsong Saga #2) * *The Devil's Dance: A Novel of Terror * Drag Thing; or, The Strange Tale of Jackle and Hyde * The Earth and All It Holds: An Historical Novel * A Family Affair: A Novel of Horror * Fatal Flowers: A Novel of Horror * Fire on the Moon: A Novel of Terror * The Gay Dogs: That Man from C.A.M.P. * The Gay Haunt * The Glass House: A Novel of Terror * The Glass Painting: A Gothic Tale of Horror * Goodbye, My Lover * The Greek Boy * The Green Rolling Hills: Writings from West Virginia* (editor) * *Green Willows: A Novel of Horror * Kenny's Back * Life & Other Passing Moments: A Collection of Short Writings * The Lion's Gate: A Novel of Terror * Love's Pawn: A Novel of Romance * Lucifer's Daughter: A Novel of Horror * Moon Garden: A Novel of Terror * Nightsong: An Historical Novel* (Nightsong Saga #1) * *The Pot Thickens: Recipes from Writers and Editors* (editor) * *San Antone: An Historical Novel * The Scent of Heather: A Novel of Terror * The Second House: A Novel of Terror * The Second Tijuana Bible Reader* (editor) * *The Sins of Nightsong: An Historical Novel* (Nightsong Saga #3) * *Spine Intact, Some Creases: Remembrances of a Paperback Writer * Stranger at the Door: A Novel of Suspense * Sweet Tormented Love: A Novel of Romance * The Sword and the Rose: An Historical Novel * This Splendid Earth: An Historical Novel * The Tijuana Bible Reader* (editor) * *Twisted Flames * The WATERCRESS File: That Man from C.A.M.P. * A Westward Love: An Historical Romance * White Jade: A Novel of Terror * The Why Not * The Wine of the Heart: A Novel of Romance * The Wolves of Craywood: A Novel of Terror*

LUCIFER'S DAUGHTER

A NOVEL OF HORROR

V. J. BANIS

THE BORGO PRESS

MMXII

FIRST BORGO PRESS EDITION

Published by Wildside Press LLC

www.wildsidebooks.com

I am deeply indebted to my friend, Heather, for all the help she has given me in getting these early works of mine reissued.

And I am grateful as well to Rob Reginald, for all his assistance and support.

CONTENTS

CHAPTER ONE

In the world there is evil.

For some, the reality of evil is hard to believe in. But this was not so for Julia Carson. Although a quiet, unassuming girl of twenty, Julia had always felt pursued by evil. It seemed to follow her wherever she went. And she sensed it now. Evil was shadowing her again. She could feel it.

A damp sea breeze brushed against the nape of her neck. Julia glanced fearfully back over her shoulder, as though fearing the presence that stood there—was always standing there—just behind her.

This is no time for bad thoughts, a bright little voice reminded her. You're on vacation, Julia. Have fun. Don't start moping. Snap out of it. This is your vacation.

Then came the other voice, the one that made her shiver, the one she knew had a sharp, cutting edge, the one she thought of as being synonymous with evil. It wasn't a voice, actually, just a dark, brooding kind of tremor that said words sometimes, and often said nothing. Usually it just stayed there inside her head trying to pull her back into its dreary recesses. She tried to ignore it; she never could.

Stop it, Julie. Don't let yourself be dragged down.

Does everyone have these voices inside them? Julia wondered, glancing at the girl on her left. Does Elizabeth? She looked to her right. Does Margaret? Does Allyson?

Neither of Julia's voices answered her. She heard nothing now, just Allyson's laughter and the jangle of loud, blaring music that came from the multicolored arcades lining the pier. The shouts, the cries of children, the mumbling voices of people having fun—she was in the dead center of all of it, yet she was not there at all. True, she was walking along an amusement pier in the seaside resort town of Paradise Bay, but she didn't feel part of it. She didn't belong here. Everything seemed so unnatural, so out of place. Dissonant chords hit uncomfortably against her ears as the pinging of a shooting gallery melted into the sounds of a merry-go-round's shrieking calliope.

The four of them stood watching the gaudy carousel spinning on its axis. Its mirrored panels flashed and danced as it whirled and spun. Its prancing stallions grinned their wide, toothy grins. The music blasted out at them as they stepped under the domed roof.

Julia held back. The deafening roar of the music, the swirling, blurring lights and shapes...she felt a pounding inside her. Her stomach gave a little tug. There was something frightening about the grotesque, painted animals, the squealing riders.

It's just a carousel.

But the other voice—the evil one—gave an ominous laugh. Julia wanted to put her hands over her ears to shut out the sound of the fiendish laugh.

"Come on, kids," Margaret called gaily. "I haven't tried for a brass ring in years."

Margaret and Allyson giggled and went toward the ticket booth.

"Come on, Julia," Elizabeth said, tugging at Julia's arm.

Julia resisted. "No, you go ahead, Liz. Those things make me dizzy. I'll only wind up sick to my stomach."

Elizabeth shrugged. "Suit yourself," she said and ran to catch up with the others.

Julia watched the three of them huddled together, giggling, gossiping. They never once looked in her direction. They waited until the carousel stopped spinning, then rushed for the flashy wooden horses that suited their personalities. Even when the merry-go-round started up and they went past her several times, none of them thought to wave or call to her. They were too busy having fun to think about her.

What am I doing here, anyway? Julia asked herself glumly. She tried hard not to watch the twirling platform. She was going to get sick if she didn't stop staring at it. But she was waiting. She was waiting for one of them—any one of them—to call out to her...to wave...anything...just some sign to say they knew she was there.

Allyson's long, blonde hair was streaming out behind her while Margaret and Elizabeth shrieked with laughter as they reached far out to snatch at the arm that fed them rings.

Maybe they'll fall off.

Stop it! Don't think such things!

Julia heard Margaret hoot. She held up a brass ring. But she didn't hold it up for Julia to see; she was showing it proudly to Allyson and Elizabeth.

Slowly Julia turned and strolled a short distance away. They didn't want to bother with her. What was she doing here with them, anyway? she asked herself again.

They're jealous of you because you're prettier than they are, the brooding, smooth voice inside her head told her.

Oh, come off it, Julia. Sure, you're pretty, but they want to have fun. They're not jealous of you. Cheer up. They like you. Everybody likes you, the other voice told her.

No, they don't. They're jealous of you. You're younger and prettier. They're jealous...jealous...jealous.

Be quiet, the other voice argued. Let the girl alone.

"Stop it, both of you," Julia shouted. Several people looked at her. Her face reddened. She turned and pretended to study an advertisement for a rock concert and fireworks display scheduled for the weekend.

Why did I come? she asked herself. They were only being polite in inviting me. They didn't want me along. Why had I accepted? They were embarrassed just because I was there when Margaret made the slip. They invited me out of politeness, that's all.

"Oh, that was fun," Allyson called as the three of them came toward her.

"You should have come along," Elizabeth said.

"I got the brass ring," Margaret put in.

"Yes, I saw," Julia answered, forcing herself to smile. "But I'm afraid those things make me dizzy. I get sick."

None of the three said anything. They went silent. Their gaiety seemed suddenly dimmed.

What did I say? Why is it a pall seems to come over everything every time I open my mouth?

"Oh, look. Candy apples. Anybody hungry?" Elizabeth asked.

Julia didn't answer. She just shook her head. She wasn't going to chance saying anything. She hated candy apples. She'd broken a tooth on one once and it ached for weeks before the people at the orphanage got around to sending her to a dentist.

"What's the matter, Julia? Don't tell me you're afraid to spoil that flawless complexion of yours?" Margaret said.

Don't take sarcasm, Julia. Tell her off, the slurring, whining voice said. Julia bit down on her lower lip. "I'm just not hungry," she managed to say.

Again the three girls dashed away and Julia was left with arguing voices that kept echoing inside her head.

She felt strange, standing there in the ebb and flow of people who moved in every conceivable direction. She just stood there and let herself be jostled by the crowd.

Her world was so far, far away from this place, she thought. And her world wasn't the chrome-and-glass skyscraper where she worked with Allyson, Elizabeth, and Margaret. Her world wasn't in that sprawling, smog-choked city with its screeching taxi cabs and snaking, dirty subway trains. She almost missed the quietness of the orphanage. She didn't miss the bad tempers and harsh punishments, but she missed the trees, the soft green grass, the sloping meadows, the lazy blue skies. What fun it would be to spend her vacation among open fields, yawning farmlands, soft, warm animals...real animals, not painted, horrible imitations that laughed and leered at her.

"Watch where you're going!"

A fat-stomached man puffing on a cigar banged into her. She hadn't been moving. She'd been standing still. *He* had bumped into *her.*

"Sorry," she said softly.

Why apologize to that big ape?

Let it go, Julia. Don't make trouble. Where's the sense to that?

"Want a bite?" Elizabeth asked, holding out the crimson apple, so hard, so shiny, so tempting. Julia thought of a snake and a garden. She shook her head.

"No, thank you."

"You feeling okay, Julie?"

"Yes, I'm fine. I'm a little bushed after that long train ride, I guess," she told Elizabeth.

"Do you want to go back to the hotel?"

Before she could answer, Allyson and Margaret were back. "What's this about going back to the hotel?" Margaret demanded.

"Julia's kind of tired."

"Julia's always kind of tired," Margaret slurred.

Tell her off, Julia. Snap her head off.

Again she bit down on her lower lip. "No, that's okay. I'm not that tired."

She saw Margaret give her a fishy look. Julia felt her hand move out. She was tempted.

Go ahead, Julia. Slap her smug little face.

No!

Julia's hand dropped to her side.

"There's a scary old roller coaster down there," Allyson said, pointing. "Anybody brave enough to try it?"

"Not me," Margaret and Elizabeth answered in unison.

Julia brightened. "Sure, why not? Come on, Ally. I'll go on it with you." She gave a little toss of her head. She couldn't trust herself to look at the astonishment on Margaret's face. She knew her own expression was one of defiance.

"You're kidding? And you're afraid of carousels?" Allyson said.

She felt Elizabeth's hand on her arm. "Are you sure, Julia?"

Julia gave a little laugh. "Sure, I'm sure. I love roller coasters."

"Have you ever ridden on one?" Elizabeth asked. Her eyes were soft and understanding. "They're pretty dangerous, you know."

Tell them you like danger.

Don't go, Julia. You'll get hurt.

Julia gave her long, dark hair a flip back over her shoulders. "I don't mind a little danger," she said with a haughtiness in her voice she'd never noticed there before. "Besides, it might liven things up a bit."

CHAPTER TWO

But the roller coaster ride didn't liven things up at all. On the contrary, Julia's stomach felt tied in knots and her head ached unmercifully. The plunging, careening ride scared her half to death, although she'd never admit it.

See, I told you not to ride on it, the soft, sympathetic little voice said.

Oh, shut up! So what's the big deal about a little upset stomach and a headache. It was fun.

You could have gotten hurt.

So what? That's what you're living for—to take chances.

Needless chances?

Julia shook her head. "Oh, quiet," she said sharply. She had gotten a little ahead of Allyson, which she blamed on her eagerness to get out of the car and away from that terrible amusement ride as quickly as possible. Allyson didn't hear her speak, but she did see her shake her head and put her hands to her temples.

"Are you all right?" Allyson asked when she caught up to Julia. They started down the ramp and headed toward where Elizabeth and Margaret were standing waiting.

"Yes, fine. My legs are a little wobbly though." She forced herself to laugh, hoping to smother the voices that were arguing inside her head.

Allyson laughed, too. "That's not all that's a little wobbly with me. Quite a ride, wasn't it?"

"It was fun." It hadn't been fun at all. She'd hated it She felt sick.

As they got nearer, Elizabeth frowned in genuine concern. "Julie. You're as white as a ghost. You shouldn't have gone on that thing."

Julia gave a little toss of her head. "I'm fine, Liz; really I am." She forced a smile. "It was wild."

"It was certainly that," Allyson agreed. She glanced at Julia. "In case you didn't know, Julie, you're supposed to scream your head off when you go down those dips. They say it helps get rid of your inhibitions."

"It would take more than screaming on a roller coaster to get rid of all my inhibitions," Julia said pleasantly enough.

"I'll buy that," Margaret interjected, with more than just a touch of sarcasm in her voice.

Julia threw her sidelong glance. She bit down on her lip and said nothing in spite of the voice inside her which was goading her to be unpleasant.

"Speaking of inhibitions," Elizabeth said, pointing to a drab little tent sitting next to a penny arcade, "there's a fortune teller over there. Let's go find out about ourselves."

"Oh, Elizabeth," Margaret said. "Surely you don't believe in fortune tellers."

Elizabeth laughed. "I believe in anyone or anything that will get me a husband."

The girls laughed gaily and started toward the tent. Julia went along, but not as eagerly as the others. There was something about the sagging, neglected little tent that seemed to warn her to stay away. But Elizabeth was pulling her along, forcing her to come with them. Julia's legs felt shaky from the unnerving effects of the roller coaster. Her head was throbbing, yet there was a lightness inside her that caused her heart to beat faster as though half expecting something wonderful and exciting to happen. She was afraid, but anxious at the same time. She felt strange, as though she was suspended between the two worlds of pleasure and pain, doubtful as to which she would be dropped into. The brooding shadow that had always followed her seemed suddenly less brooding. She knew she should stay away from the tent and the dark-complexioned gypsy woman seated before it, her hands folded contentedly in her lap, but Julia found she could not. She blamed it all on Elizabeth's firm grip on her arm. They were forcing her to go into the tent and there was nothing she could do about it.

The old gypsy's weather-beaten face turned on them as they approached. A trace of a smile tickled the mouth, but the eyes weren't smiling. The eyes were cold and dark and the color of death. She greeted the girls, letting her eyes take each of them in as they came to stand before her. Julia was standing slightly behind Elizabeth. The old gypsy's eyes widened as though in recognition when she looked deep into Julia's face, but the woman said nothing. Then, with an obvious move to compose herself, the gypsy got slowly to her feet, carefully avoiding looking at Julia again.

What had she seen? Julia wondered. She seemed to recognize me from somewhere, but Julia had never laid eyes on the woman in her life.

The gypsy cleared her throat in a nervous gesture and said, "Well, my pretty things, can I tell you what man lurks in each of your futures?" Her eyes traveled from face to face again, but did not venture as far as Julia's face.

"How much do you charge?" Margaret wanted to know.

"Private readings are five dollars."

"Five dollars. Oh, wow, that's too much," Allyson complained.

The old gypsy chuckled. "However, if you don't mind knowing each other's secrets, I can do a group reading for eight."

Allyson, Margaret, and Elizabeth went into a hurried conference. Again Julia felt unwanted. They had automatically assumed that she had no intention of including herself in their adventure. She felt perturbed, but did not push herself into their whispered discussion. The girls agreed that eight dollars was reasonable enough.

Then Elizabeth turned to Julia. "Do you want to be included? It'll only cost you two dollars."

"Yes, come on, Julia. Don't be such a stick-in-the-mud,"

Margaret insisted.

So that was it, Julia told herself. They weren't all that interested in including her except one more added to the group session would bring the price down.

However, it wasn't spite alone that tempted her to refuse them. For reasons she could not explain, she didn't want to learn about her future. She felt she had no future...not even a future manufactured from the experienced imagination of an old gypsy woman. Ever since she could remember, the future seemed to be meant for everyone else but her.

Strange, now that she thought of it, how unimportant the coming years seemed. Nothing had ever lain in store for her. The present was all that had ever existed and all that would ever continue to exist. She lived from day to day, never for tomorrow, because there were no tomorrows. Time was a dimension that mattered little. She lived in a vacuum. Only emptiness lay behind her; nothing lay ahead. Looking back over everything, she seemed to have spent her life waiting for something to complete her existence. What she waited for she did not know, but she felt she must wait. There was no place for her in the lives of others, and she had no desire to clutter up her own life with friendships she knew she could not afford.

Why she had bothered to come with Allyson, Elizabeth, and Margaret she didn't know. It had been a drastic mistake. She should have known better. Whenever she made a spur-of-the-moment decision, it always proved wrong. She was sorry she'd come. She wanted to go back to her little furnished apartment in the city where she could be alone with her troubled thoughts and the unnerving voices that constantly talked to her.

She stood there deep in her own thoughts, oblivious of the three girls who were trying to coax her to join them. Elizabeth gave her arm a hard tug. It brought Julia back to the present. She saw the old gypsy woman looking at her again. She remembered the woman's first look of astonishment, of recognition. Perhaps the gypsy really did know something about Julia that would benefit her. Despite all her resolve to refuse the others, she found herself giving in. She let Elizabeth pull her inside the tent.

Once inside, Julia saw another expression pass over the gypsy's face. It was one of disapproval. The old woman looked none too pleased with Julia for having joined the others. Julia found herself tossing back a look of defiance and seated herself with the girls around a draped table, in the center of which sat a crystal ball.

The gypsy did not take her place at the table until the matter of payment was dispensed with. Each girl contributed her share, which the old woman collected. She carried the bills into a deeper recess of the eerily lighted tent. She reappeared a moment later.

"Well," the old gypsy said with a heavy sigh as she settled herself opposite the girls. She leaned over the crystal ball which glowed with a strange light.

The gypsy looked again from one to the other of the girls, giving Julia only the briefest glance. "I must explain," the old woman started. "In group readings, it is necessary for me to put myself into a trance from which I cannot emerge until all the readings are completed. After I have passed over into my hypnotic state, each of you will take turns placing your hands, palms down, on the table, extended toward the crystal ball. Above all else, do not touch the crystal ball, just put your hands close enough to it for it to pick up the heat of your body. Whatever I say will be directed to the person whose hands are on the table. Only one pair of hands must be on the table at a time, otherwise the powers of darkness will become confused and the communication muddied and garbled. Do you understand? Good. Then we can begin." The old woman closed her eyes and tilted her head back. Her lips moved, but emitted no sounds. Slowly her wrinkled and bony hands raised up, as though in supplication, and the woman began to speak.

"Hear me, great powers from beyond this world. Tell me what is in store for this young beauty."

The tent suddenly dropped into darkness. The girls all tittered and looked around. After a moment they settled themselves and Allyson placed her hands palms down on the table, extending them close to the glowing crystal ball.

The gypsy's eyes opened wide, but they stared, unseeing, at the darkness around them. "I invoke and command thee, O spirit, by all the resplendent and potent names of the great and unparalleled Azliel, to come here to this place instanter. Come from whichever place thou art and give answers to my questions. Come in visible or invisible form. Come and speak pleasantly in words I may understand."

Julia, unlike the others, was looking around for signs of trickery. She expected to see a vague shape take form in the sudden blackness, which she was convinced was obtained through the benefit of electric switches located beneath the table. However, no shimmering, unearthly shape appeared. Nothing floated through the space over their heads. No drafts of cold air tickled the backs of their necks. Julia frowned her disappointment.

The tent was deadly quiet for several long, ominous moments. Then the gypsy's lips moved again but her voice was not her own. She spoke in a man's voice, a voice so unreal and so unnatural the girls, including Julia, gasped and stared in disbelief.

"What will you have me tell you?" the voice asked.

"This girl. Her name is Alice...no, Allyson. She wishes to know what her future holds in store." This time the old woman spoke in her own voice.

Another long, eerie silence followed. Then the mysterious man's voice said, "She will marry soon. She will meet her betrothed on a beach. They will fall in love and will live in happiness forever."

A little cry of pleasure went out of Allyson. She turned to Margaret, who was seated beside her. They looked at each other, saying nothing, too surprised to speak. After a second or two Allyson turned back and stared at the crystal ball and waited for the voice to continue. When it did not, she took her hands from the table. "The old gypsy knew my name," Allyson whispered.

"How could she know my name?"

Margaret shrugged. "She obviously heard us talking among ourselves. We mentioned each other's names, I suppose."

"Oh, it's kinda exciting," Allyson gushed. "You can bet your last dollar I'll be on the beach tomorrow bright and early."

The girls giggled.

"She didn't say you'd meet him tomorrow, Ally," Margaret told her.

Allyson smothered a laugh. "I know, but I intend to start looking as soon as I can." Between giggles Allyson nudged Margaret. "Go ahead, Maggie. Put your hands on the table. Let's see what she has to say about you."

Margaret hesitated, then remembered her two-dollar investment and put her hands palms down in front of her.

Allyson nodded toward the crystal ball and Margaret stretched her hands closer to it.

The old woman was seated, staring upward, seemingly unaware that there were others near her. The moment Margaret's hands touched the table top the old gypsy's lips began to quiver.

"Your name...your name...," the old woman said.

Margaret said nothing.

"Your name is Margaret." The gypsy paused. "Tell us, O great spirit, what is in store for this girl?"

"Margaret," the man's voice droned. "Margaret. Be careful of vehicles. Be careful of your money. Your future is uncertain unless your ways are changed now."

"Will I marry?" Margaret asked, ignoring the warnings. "That's all I'm interested in knowing."

"Love will come easily to you, Margaret," the man's voice said. "You will find it too often, and each time it will bring with it great unhappiness. You will marry three times."

"I hope they'll all be rich," Margaret scoffed, pulling her hands back from the table.

"Oh, Maggie, you shouldn't make light of it. You'll break the trance and we won't hear what she has to say about Elizabeth and Julie."

"Oh, phooey," Margaret huffed. "You surely don't believe all this bunk?"

"Hush," Allyson cautioned, still pleased with her own prediction for the future. "Go ahead, Julie. You go next."

Julia held back. "N—no," she stammered, "I don't think I want to."

"I'll go," Elizabeth said eagerly, putting her hands down on the table.

The girls settled themselves into quietness and waited, all except Margaret who was beginning to get restless. Allyson nudged her and whispered for her to be still.

The voice took longer this time, but finally it came from the old woman's lips.

"Elizabeth, you have much happiness awaiting you. You will leave your present place of employment shortly and will work for a young executive who will fall in love with you and you with him. You will marry before a year has passed."

Elizabeth hooted and clasped her hands to her breast. She giggled across Margaret to Allyson who also clapped her hands with glee. "Oh, Liz, how exciting." They gushed among themselves for a few moments, then turned their eyes on Julia.

"Okay, Julia," Margaret said irritably. "Hurry up and let's get this over with."

"Oh, don't be such a grouch, Maggie. What are you grousing about? You're going to have three husbands to Ally's and my one," Elizabeth said. Then she turned to Julia. "Go ahead, Julie. Let's see when and where you're going to meet your Prince Charming."

Julia pulled back. What she had to fear she didn't know, but there was a strange throbbing deep inside her that was telling her to get out of that tent, to get away from the mysterious voice and the glowing crystal ball that seemed to pulse and radiate from the center of the table.

"Oh, go on, Julie," Allyson urged. "You might just as well get your money's worth."

"Sure, Julie. Go ahead. Please," Elizabeth insisted.

Reluctantly Julia let Elizabeth lift her hands onto the table. She put them palms down and moved them toward the crystal ball.

The old woman sat there in silence, her lips still and unmoving. Elizabeth nudged Julia and pushed her hands closer to the glowing crystal ball.

The old crone sat for a moment longer, then she stirred and her lips moved. "The girl is Julia," she said. She paused. Her head started to move back and forth, slowly at first and then with more and more deliberateness. "No. The girl is called...," she stammered. "The girl's name is not Julia."

Allyson, Margaret, and Elizabeth turned and stared at Julia. But Julia was suddenly gazing deep into the crystal ball, entranced, waiting for something of which she was deathly afraid. But she was too frozen to move.

Julia felt a hot, wet mist envelop her. Out of the corner of her eye she saw him standing just over her shoulder. The air inside the tent grew thicker and heavier. She couldn't move. She couldn't cry out. Something, someone was holding shut her mouth and had made her limbs immobile. An unearthly silence descended on her. She felt herself being pressed deeper and deeper into the earth between her feet. She felt herself sinking into oblivion. Silence—dead, thick, heavy silence—permeated the place. Not a breath of air stirred as she sat there waiting... waiting...waiting.

Suddenly the old woman groaned. Her tired, ageless eyes went wide with terror. "No!" she shrieked. "No! Go away!" Her head fell back, her eyes dropped closed. Then her body went rigid. "No—" she shrieked again. "Go away! Go away!" She waved her hands in front of her as if warding off a swarm of locusts. "Go! Leave me! Go! Go!"

Then with an agonizing moan, her body swayed and toppled backward. She fell unconscious to the floor.

Three of the girls screamed. Julia sat engulfed in her stupor. She just stared into the crystal ball. Then, with a dull thud, the ball in the center of the table shattered into fragments.

Julia moaned. Then, like the old gypsy, she fell into a dead faint.

CHAPTER THREE

When her eyelids fluttered and opened, Julia saw she was still inside the tent. It was lit more brightly now, and her three companions were clustered around her. Elizabeth was patting her wrists. Allyson had managed to find a towel and some cold water which she was applying to Julia's forehead. Margaret just stood looking down with obvious disapproval.

"She's coming round," Elizabeth said.

"Thank goodness. Julie. Julie," Allyson said softly. "Are you all right?"

"What happened?"

"You fainted."

"Oh, yes, I remember," Julia tried to focus on her surroundings. She saw the dreary interior and the draped table. Her eyes lingered on the shattered pieces of crystal that lay scattered on the cloth. She did not want to stay here; the place represented something bad, something evil. From out of nowhere the words someone had called to her returned: "Evil!" No, she could not stay here. She had to get away.

She tried to sit up but Elizabeth eased her back. "Rest for a minute. The gypsy woman has gone to get the park's nurse."

"No, please," Julia protested. "I don't want a nurse. I'm fine. I just want to get out of here."

"You must rest, Julie. You're obviously not well."

"I had a simple dizzy spell. I suppose it was the after-effects of that roller coaster ride." She knew perfectly well it was not the roller coaster ride that had made her faint. It had been something very different. Precisely what had caused her to pass out she couldn't be certain. Everything was fuzzy inside her head. She rubbed her temples. She tried to think of what had happened to her, but for a time nothing registered except the word "evil" being repeated over and over inside her brain.

Who had called her evil? What had happened? She thought back, forcing her mind to retrace as much time as it could. In the distance she heard the music of the carousel and remembered standing watching it spinning and spinning, waiting for the girls to wave to her. She remembered the terror that gripped her as the car of the roller coaster roared and raced up and down and around its tracks, its screeching, clanging wheels propelling them to speeds faster than the wind.

Cautiously she turned her memory to the old gypsy woman. She began to tremble inside. It had been the old gypsy woman who'd called her evil. She remembered now. She had said Julia Carson was not her real name. Gradually everything started to shift back into perspective.

"A face," she said aloud. She sat up, pushing Elizabeth away. "There was a man's face in the crystal ball...and then it shattered."

"You obviously knocked it off its little pedestal," Allyson said. "It cracked and fell into several pieces."

"I'll bet anything that old gypsy will insist you pay for it," Margaret said, sounding disgruntled.

"Oh, Margaret," Elizabeth admonished. "The gypsy will expect no such thing. Poor thing fainted too," she added, turning back to Julia. "Do you remember, Julie? She wasn't passed out very long, however. She stirred almost immediately. Then, when she saw you with your head on the table, she told us to lift you over onto this divan and she rushed out to find the nurse."

Allyson dabbed Julia's forehead. "What do you suppose the gypsy meant when she said your name wasn't Julia?" she asked.

Julia frowned. "Yes, I remember her telling me that. I don't know what she could have meant." Julia purposely laughed, hoping to make light of the situation. "Of course, you all know

I was an orphan, so my real name could have been anything."

"How did the old gypsy know you were an orphan?" Margaret asked.

Julia shrugged and tried to look indifferent. "I think she recognized me when we walked over to her tent. They used to bring entertainers like her up to the orphanage to entertain the children. Maybe she remembered me from there."

"But when people adopt, don't they usually keep the baby's first name, at least?" Allyson asked.

"Julia wasn't adopted," Margaret said, seeming to remind Julia that no one had wanted her.

"No, that's true," Julia said. "The people at the orphanage don't usually change a baby's name if it has one to start with."

Elizabeth brightened. "Ah, then that's probably what the gypsy was referring to. She remembered you from the orphanage and she just presumed that your parents had died or abandoned you and you had a name on a birth certificate somewhere that was different from the name the orphanage gave you. She might have surmised that you were just a foundling."

Margaret chuckled. "The old woman just made up the whole thing, if you want my opinion."

"I never was told whether Julia Carson was my real name or not," Julia said. "They never told me how I came to be an orphan. They just kept me until I was eighteen, then kicked me out." She tried to laugh but the laugh did not come. She didn't feel much like laughing. "They won't tell the orphans much about themselves, especially the older ones like myself. They don't want them to go out scouring the bushes in hopes of finding their parents. We all like to think we were not abandoned, just lost somewhere...that we were never consciously given up by our mothers and fathers. Nobody likes to think of themselves as having been an unwanted child."

There was a moment of uncomfortable silence as each of them struggled with their guilt and uneasiness. Even Margaret held her tongue.

The silence was broken when the gypsy came into the tent

followed by a rather large woman dressed in white. Elizabeth had made it seem that the gypsy was worried and concerned about Julia. One look at the old gypsy's face told Julia that the woman felt neither worry nor concern for her. Her eyes were narrowed in anger and her mouth was drawn tight against her teeth. Her expression could only be defined as one of open hostility.

"Get her out of here," the gypsy ordered, pointing a menacing finger at Julia. "You must take her away. Take her out of my sight!"

"Now, now," the nurse said. "Let's not get ourselves all excited." She ignored the fuming gypsy and came over to Julia. She felt her forehead, brushing back several loose strands of hair that had fallen forward. "I understand you fainted, dear."

Julia nodded. "Yes." She rubbed her temples again. "I don't know why exactly. I'd been on the roller coaster with Allyson and I suppose the ride made me dizzy." She glanced at Allyson who smiled at her. "And it was so warm and dark inside this tent."

The nurse laid her fingers to Julia's pulse. "Are you feeling all right now?"

"Oh, yes. I'm feeling much better."

"Get her out of here," the gypsy demanded."She is trouble."

Julia shot her a frightened look. "Trouble? Why do you say that?"

"You are trouble. I see terrible things." The old woman put her hands over her eyes. "I do not want to remember. You are evil. Go away. Take her out of my sight!"

The nurse glanced from the gypsy to Julia. She smiled reassuringly. "I suppose if you are feeling well enough, we could walk you over to my first-aid station. You could rest there if you wish. Your presence here seems to be upsetting Madam Esperelda."

"I'll just go along back to my hotel," Julia said. "I don't need to rest. I'll be all right."

The nurse helped Julia to her feet. Julia still felt a bit faint and not too steady, but she forced herself to stand tall and straight. Leaning slightly on the nurse's arm, she walked out of the tent with Elizabeth, Allyson, and Margaret following silently. As Julia passed the old gypsy woman she turned and looked at her. The old crone's face was black and somber. She recoiled from Julia's gaze. The gypsy raised her shawl up to hide her face from Julia's eyes. "Go away," she said in a frightened voice.

"Please," Julia implored. "You are making terrible accusations of me. You must tell me what you mean. What did the crystal ball tell you?"

"Go. Leave me. Go."

Julia felt miserable standing there, knowing she was frightening the old woman. The others had heard everything. Their faces were registering exactly what they thought. Every one of them would carry away this new stigma that had been so unjustly put on her.

She sighed, admitting her feelings of inferiority to herself. Now Elizabeth and Allyson and Margaret had still another reason to exclude her from their friendships. She had been singled out as being an evil person, a troublemaker. Elizabeth, of course, would say it was merely the ravings of a silly old gypsy woman, but deep down she'd hang on to those ravings and would let them color their relationship. Allyson would treat her more indifferently than before. She would smile and say she understood, but she'd retain that cool indifference she always had. And Margaret...well, Margaret would openly display her dislike for Julia.

Julia's heart was sinking. The vacation she'd put so much faith in had turned into a disaster. It would be useless to keep up appearances now. She'd tell them she was going home tomorrow. She knew she could never stay. She knew that to them she represented a hovering, black, damp cloud. She'd only make their vacation miserable. Yes, she'd go home tomorrow, she decided.

Once outside in the clear night air, the smell of the sea and the feeling of the cold, salty breeze helped revive her somewhat. The old gypsy's words continued to press on her, but now that she was away from the tent the words seemed less ominous. She stopped and turned back to look toward the tent. The nurse patted her hand. "Come along, dear. The first-aid station is just over here."

"Excuse me," Julia said, easing herself from the nurse's support. "I really am feeling quite all right. I do appreciate your concern, but I don't think I need trouble you any longer. I'm fine now, really I am."

The nurse cocked her head and looked skeptical. Just then a man came hurrying toward them. "Nurse," he called, "a little boy just fell off the carousel. You'd better come quick."

The nurse's skepticism about leaving Julia vanished immediately. "I'll get my bag, Hank," she said as she started away. Then she stopped and turned back. "You're sure you're all right, honey?" she asked Julia.

"Yes, fine. You'd better hurry. The boy might be seriously hurt. Don't worry about me."

The nurse gave a quick nod and hurried off.

"Well," Margaret breathed. "I suppose we'll have to see *the evil one here* back to the hotel before she gets into any more trouble."

Julia forced herself to be pleasant. "No, please," she protested. "Please don't bother about me. I don't want to spoil your fun. You three go along. I can find my way back."

"Oh, no, Julie," Elizabeth said. "We'll come with you."

"Why?" Margaret asked. "Julia said she could navigate under her own steam. Why do we have to go with her? All she's going to do is go to bed. I'm sure she can manage that without our help."

Julia forced herself to smile. "Of course I can. Please, Liz, go along. I can manage. I'm really feeling quite all right. Honest I am."

Elizabeth hesitated. "You're sure?"

"I'm sure. Go along with the others. I insist."

Margaret was the first to walk away. She walked to the far side of the boardwalk and stood looking out at the ocean. Allyson turned, but a little reluctantly. She glanced back at Julia. "Don't pay any attention to that silly old gypsy woman," Allyson said. "Get into bed, Julie. I'm sorry I suggested that roller coaster ride." Then she too hurried away, going toward Margaret at the rail.

It was Elizabeth who stood there debating with herself. "Oh, really, Julie. I feel terrible about all this. I insist I come with you back to the hotel. You may have another dizzy spell. You shouldn't be left alone."

"Please, Liz. I'd rather be by myself. You go along with the others." She glanced toward Margaret and Allyson. "Don't keep them waiting."

Julia waited until the three had walked out of sight. She had no intention of returning to the hotel. The woolly mess had cleared up inside her head and she was thinking rationally again. And with the return of her rationality came the return of her strange little voices. She hadn't realized they'd deserted her during her ordeal with the gypsy fortune teller until they started bickering among themselves. She wanted them to stop because their wrangling was interfering with her resolve.

Forcing herself to ignore them, she fumbled in her purse and made certain she had what she needed. With hurrying steps she went back in the direction from which she'd come.

The old gypsy wasn't seated outside the tent. Julia found her huddled over the shattered crystal ball. She was mumbling to herself and handling the crystal fragments as though they were precious diamonds. Julia stood just inside the tent flap, waiting for the old woman to acknowledge her presence. When she did not, Julia cleared her throat.

The old crone looked up. When she saw Julia standing there, she gave a start and got to her feet so quickly that the stool on which she had been sitting tipped over backward. The gypsy averted her eyes and swept her arm. "Go away."

"You must tell me what you saw," Julia insisted.

"No. I cannot. I will not. Go. Go."

"You called me evil. You say I am trouble. You've embarrassed me in front of my friends and even a stranger, and now you refuse to explain. I have no intention of going anywhere until you tell me what you believe to have seen."

"I saw what I saw. It was real enough. It was evil. You are evil."

Julia glowered at her. "Stop saying that! Tell me what you saw in that crystal ball. Why did it shatter?"

"It shattered from the impact of the evil that was implanted into its depth. You brought Him into it."

"Him?" Julia frowned at her, remembering vaguely the image of the man's face reflected in the dim glow of the ball. "Who was he? Who was the man?"

"I cannot tell you that."

"You must. It was my future you saw. It had to do with me. I paid your fee. You owe it to me."

"Go away, child," the gypsy said, her voice softening. Her words came out more in the tone of a plea than an order.

Julia fumbled in her handbag and pulled out a large bill. "You must help me. Here, take this and tell me whatever it was you saw."

The old woman looked at the bill. Her hand trembled, then moved toward it. Suddenly she snatched her hand back. "No. You must never know the evil that lurks in your future. I cannot tell you. I *will* not tell you. It is for your own sake."

"I saw a strange man's face in the crystal just before it shattered. Also, there was someone—a man—standing just behind me while you were entranced. Was it a trick you employed? You must tell me if this is all trickery. I must know."

The gypsy shook her head. "There is no trickery here. You saw what you saw. I cannot vouch for any strange being who might have taken shape near you. I have nothing to do with conjurations; they can only be accomplished by your own patterns of thought and with your own mind power...or by those more powerful than I."

Julia pulled another bill from her purse and shoved it into the gypsy's hand. "If you will not help me, then please tell me who can. You see, I have never had a father or mother. My past is a blank. You are the first person who has given me any insight into my real self. All my life I have wondered who I was or what I am. You say I am evil. You say I am trouble. If that be the case, then at least put me on the right path so that I may be given the opportunity to avoid the evil you say I will do, the trouble I will cause. Help me. You must. You have the power. Please, help me."

The gypsy woman had been staring down at the dirt floor. When Julia finished her plea, the old woman slowly raised her eyes and gazed into Julia's. She stared at her for several full minutes.

"When I first laid my eyes on you," the gypsy said, "I felt I'd seen you before somewhere, and I was afraid. I do not know why. There is something in your eyes to fear. I wanted nothing to do with you. The image in the crystal ball confirmed my fears. But now that I look upon you again I see yet another face...a face that does not disturb me. You are another girl suddenly. You seem to be the personification of both good and evil. Which is the stronger of the two, I do not know. That is for you to determine."

The old woman stared more closely into Julia's eyes. "I believe I know someone who might help you." Her eyes wandered away, as though debating as to whether she should continue. They returned quickly. "Yes," the gypsy decided. "I will send you to someone who will be able to direct you. Perhaps that will not be an easy path to follow, but she will show you the way, and you will then have to decide for yourself." The gypsy turned and went toward the back of the tent. She disappeared behind a canvas partition.

Julia shook her head. She wasn't an evil person. She had never caused anyone any trouble. Yet, as she thought back over her young life, she began remembering those many, many individuals who had shied away from her. She had never succeeded in befriending anyone except for an occasional frightened little child who was in her charge at the orphanage. But once she befriended them, the matrons always removed the charges from her care. Perhaps all those people who avoided her saw something in her that she did not know was there. Perhaps others saw what the old gypsy had seen.

Was she an evil being? she began to wonder. She'd often felt evil just behind her, but she thought she'd managed to keep ahead of it at all times. Perhaps it had finally caught up with her.

The seeds of doubt were planted. She'd have to find out the true nature of those seeds before permitting them to bear fruit, she told herself.

CHAPTER FOUR

A ramshackle old house sat at the farthermost end of a cul-de-sac. The hour was late and the fog rolling in from the sea made the place look brooding and ominous. Julia sat in the back seat of the taxi with the little piece of paper the gypsy had given her. She glanced down and then up at the house number, confirming that she was at the right place.

"Do you want me to wait?" the cab driver asked.

"Yes, perhaps it would be a good idea. There doesn't seem to be anyone at home...at least there aren't any lights that I can see." She got out of the cab and started across the crooked pavement and up the wooden steps to the porch. The flooring was sagging and warped, the fog swirled around, making every step soundless. The bushes and shrubs had advanced in such unchecked profusion they obscured any light on the lower level from view.

Once on the porch, Julia saw a dim light that burned in one of the large downstairs windows.

What was she doing here? Why had she come to this desolate place? What had she hoped to discover about herself that she didn't know already? Elizabeth had been right. The old gypsy had just been playacting, and now she was sending Julia to some friend or cohort who would more than likely try to coax Julia into giving up more of her hard-earned money.

Julia pressed the button alongside the door. The door creaked open. Julia found herself holding her breath. At first she saw nothing, only a dim light and empty space.

"Yes?" a voice said.

Julia looked down in the direction of the voice and saw a face peering up at her. The flame of a candle flickered just below the plump chin, making the face seem disconnected from its body. She thought at first it was a child, but the eyes were old and the cheeks puffed and yellow with age. Heavy sacks of skin hung from beneath the smoldering eyes. Julia felt her blood begin to race more quickly through her veins.

"Madam Esperelda told me you might help me," Julia managed to say. She found her voice trembling.

"What kind of help do you need?"

Julia hesitated. "I don't know." She couldn't think of anything to say. She held out the slip of paper the gypsy had given her. "Madam Esperelda sent me to you."

The face that floated in the crack between door and jamb frowned. "Come in," the woman said quickly.

"I have a taxi waiting," Julia said, glancing over her shoulder. "I wasn't sure anyone would be at home."

The eyes just looked up at her; they said nothing.

"If I send him away, do you have a telephone which I could use to call for another taxi?"

The head floating above the flame of the candle nodded.

Hurriedly, as if anxious to get away from the strange, rather frightening little face, Julia went back down the steps, paid the driver, and thanked him for his patience. When she returned to the porch, the face was still hovering there. Then Julia heard invisible fingers undo a safety chain and the door swung open.

The interior into which Julia stepped was more depressing than the outside of the old house. The hall was heavy with draperies, furniture, rugs, pictures, wallpaper, dark paneling, cluttered tables. A staircase of shiny, black ebony ran up one wall.

A pair of amber eyes stared down at her from halfway up the stairs. The eyes stayed steadily fixed on her. Then Julia saw movement and the eyes vanished. She recognized the shape of a huge cat disappearing on the upper landing.

The woman motioned Julia into a room on the right. The room, like the hall, was overloaded with too many furnishings.

All of the tables wore shawls, every surface was cluttered with objects of all descriptions. There wasn't a single inch of wall space showing between picture frames, tapestries, and hangings of all sorts. The windows were shrouded in heavy, blue-black velvet. Wax candles flickered and smoked.

The woman nodded toward a chair, complete with antimacassars, throw pillows, and footstool. Julia perched herself on the very edge of its sagging cushion.

"What seems to be troubling you, girl?" the woman asked as she settled herself on a chair with a flowered slipcover, ruffled bottom, and wide, drooping arms. She propped her plump little fingers under her chin and fixed her eyes on Julia. She resembled a hungry cat contemplating a meal. The thought made Julia shift uneasily.

"I fainted when Madam Esperelda began reading my fortune," Julia said in a rush. She wanted to get it all out and over with. She decided she'd made a mistake coming to this strange little woman. The place frightened her; the woman frightened her. "The gypsy said she saw something evil in my fortune. When I looked into her crystal ball, it shattered into pieces." Julia was studying her own hands; she found she could not look into the woman's face.

At this last bit of information, the woman's hand went away from her chin. Her plump little head came straight up. She pushed herself erect and leaned forward, staring hard into Julia's face. "The crystal shattered, you say?"

"Yes. I saw a man's face reflected dimly in it...at least I think it was a man's face...and then it broke into pieces. That was when I fainted. Madam Esperelda fainted, too," she added, almost as an afterthought.

"Hmmmmm." The woman's head lowered and she studied Julia from under her drooping eyelids. "And you want to know what made the crystal shatter?"

"I want to know why the gypsy said she saw evil in me. The face and the man who stood beside me could have been some sort of trick...I don't care about them, I only want to...."

"A man stood beside you?" the woman asked, frowning with interest.

"Yes. I saw the face in the glass, and there was a man standing just behind me. I think it was his face that was reflected in the crystal ball."

The woman put a plump little finger into her mouth and began chewing on it. She thought hard for a moment, then nodded and rolled her eyes. "I see. I see," she mumbled.

"What do you see?"

"Nothing, girl. Nothing." She went silent.

"I really don't like someone calling me evil," Julia said a little boldly. "She had no right to make such terrible accusations. I'm an orphan, you see, and I know nothing about my past. Things such as this upset me, I'm afraid. Knowing nothing about one's origin—"

"I understand, child. I understand," the woman mumbled, waving a hand to silence Julia. She thought for a moment, then said, "You must return after I have been able to make the necessary arrangements for a séance. That is the only way we will be able to find out whatever is to be found out."

"What does it all mean?" Julia asked.

"Well, from what little you've told me, I would suspect you had a visitation."

"Visitation?" Julia frowned. "From whom?"

The woman shrugged her stocky little shoulders. "It might have been anyone," she said. "But in view of the crystal ball shattering and Madam Esperelda's vision of evil and trouble, I would say you were visited by Satan himself."

Julia gasped. "Oh, I just can't see how such a thing is possible."

"It is not nonsense, child, you can believe me...I know. You are not the first the Lord of Darkness has deigned to honor with a visit."

"Honor? I want no part of demons or devils."

"But the Master is no one to fear, girl. Not many people are as fortunate as you have been, as much as they wish for it."

Julia's stomach tightened. Surely the woman wasn't serious, she thought. No one in their right senses would welcome a visit from Satan himself. She said as much to the woman seated across from her.

Surprisingly, Julia heard the woman laugh softly. "But why shouldn't it be an honor to be visited by one of such esteem? After all, he is an angel...a supreme being."

"A fallen angel," Julia corrected. "He's the personification of evil."

"Ah, but there are many kinds of evil, just as there are many kinds of goodness. Goodness can sometimes be evil. Lucifer has the power of doing much good for his worthy disciples. He has the power to grant happiness, health, prosperity, joy. There is nothing he cannot grant. We who are knowledgeable in the world of the black arts do not look upon Lucifer as evil. He is a spirit just like any other, but he is an extremely powerful and magnificent spirit, deserving of every courtesy and sacrifice."

"But I am not one of his disciples. Why should he choose to appear to me, if that is what you believe he did?"

"That is something we must find out. I will hold a séance. Perhaps he will reappear and make his desires known. Perhaps not." She put her hands on her knees and pushed herself up out of the chair. "You will return tomorrow night at eight o'clock. Wear no jewelry and put on a simple black dress if you have one, otherwise anything plain and of a dark color will suffice, but black preferably. I will have the others present."

"Others?"

"The Devil's number is four and four. We will have six souls combine with ours tomorrow evening. You and I are not powerful enough alone to make the journey to the other side."

Julia got to her feet. "I'll be here at eight tomorrow night." She hesitated and frowned. It was almost as if someone else had spoken for her.

"Good," the woman said, nodding her head slowly.

Julia glanced down at the slip of paper she still held in her hand. "I'm afraid I don't know your name," she said. "Madam

Esperelda supplied me with only your address."

"That is as it should be. Remember, I do not know your name either. We will be introduced if it is necessary." She turned and started out of the room. "The telephone is here in the hall. You'll find the number of the cab company written on the pad."

I won't come back, Julia told herself—but another part of her knew that was not true.

CHAPTER FIVE

"Julie, you look lovely," Elizabeth said when Julia came out of the bathroom wearing her trim black dress.

"You should have pearls to set it off," Allyson said.

"I'm afraid I didn't remember to pack them."

Margaret frowned. She'd packed one good dress and a strand of pearls, but she had no intention of loaning the pearls to Julia.

Julia glanced briefly at her reflection in the mirror. She hadn't told the girls her true destination. They seemed excited for her, albeit a little envious. Margaret showed her jealousy more openly than the others. They were convinced Julia had a date with a man; Julia did not elaborate on her invitation out. All she had said was that she'd met someone who'd asked if they could see her this evening. She didn't feel she was lying by letting the girls jump to their own, incorrect conclusions.

"I'd better dash," Julia said as again she glanced at her watch. "Don't wait up," she tossed back over her shoulder.

"Be careful, Julie," Elizabeth warned. Julia recognized the hint of genuine concern in Liz's voice. Of the three, Elizabeth was the most thoughtful of her...but Elizabeth was thoughtful of everyone, even people she disliked.

Julia found a cab just outside the hotel. She glanced at her watch again. The medium's house wasn't far. She'd make it in plenty of time. She gave the address to the driver and remembered to unclip her wristwatch and drop it into her bag. She leaned back against the seat but found she couldn't relax. She felt suddenly nervous, not knowing what she might be getting herself involved in. She tried to calm herself by telling herself that it was nothing more than a new and exciting adventure. It was different and it would be amusing, if nothing else. She reminded herself that a group of people were getting together for her sake alone. The thought was pleasant enough, although slightly unnerving.

At two minutes to eight the taxi pulled up in front of the house at the end of the cul-de-sac. The place looked less forlorn tonight. Oddly enough, Julia thought as she paid the driver, there was a certain warmth about the place now. It seemed to be looking down at her as though welcoming an old friend. She found her steps lighter, springier, as she went up onto the porch and pressed the doorbell.

She had expected the medium to answer her ring and was surprised when a man opened the door.

"Good evening. I'm Julia Carson. I believe I'm expected."

He smiled. "Indeed you are," he said, "but the introduction wasn't necessary. My aunt prefers to work without benefit of knowing anything about a new subject." He opened the door wider and ushered her in. "She feels that facts complicate her purpose."

He was a pleasant-looking man, Julia noted, of about thirty-five, no more than thirty-eight, with bright, blue eyes, and a thick wave of jet-black hair that hung well down over his brow.

He smiled at her. "Not being a medium myself," he said with a slight glint in his expression, "I personally approve of introductions, especially when a beautiful young lady is involved." He held out his hand. "I'm Fred McAndrews."

His grasp was strong and friendly. "How do you do."

He nodded toward a closed doorway. "My aunt and the others are waiting for us in there."

He opened the door for her and Julia entered a different room than the one she'd seen the night before. This room was lighted by electricity and not candles but was just as cluttered, although it was a different kind of clutter. The walls were adorned with the most unusual paintings and designs Julia had ever seen.

There were mysterious symbols and markings of varied sizes, descriptions and colors. One wall was covered with a painting of a huge bird of unrecognizable ancestry. Tiny faces peered out from its outstretched wings. Its claws were curled around naked forms of no particular sex. The head of this massive creature was painted a brilliant yellow with blood-red eyes and beak. Around its neck was a chain of what looked like door keys, and on its plumed breast rested a medallion which, on closer inspection, Julia noticed was not painted but an actual piece of jewelry beset with gems (obviously not genuine) of red and yellow and blue and black.

The ceiling, too, was painted with designs and bizarre pictures, the most dominating figure being that of the head of a golden bull or calf.

A large, round table sat in the middle of the room, with eight chairs spaced evenly around its edge. Six of the chairs were occupied, and when Fred McAndrews seated himself, only the chair at the far end remained vacant. The short, plump little woman of yesterday sat chatting with the others gathered around her. When Julia was ushered into the room, the medium looked up and smiled. She motioned Julia to the remaining empty chair between a handsomely dressed matron wearing an expensive black fur and a rather frail-looking young man wearing a blousy black silk shirt and a black velvet ribbon tied around his throat. Both the matron and the frail young man smiled at her as she took her place between them.

"The social amenities can take place following our séance," the medium told Julia. "I prefer not knowing anything about you at first, my dear. Facts clutter up my vibrations."

Julia nodded. Her eyes wandered briefly in Fred McAndrews direction. He smiled at her. She felt herself blush and shifted her eyes back to the medium.

"Now, if you are all relaxed and composed, we can begin." The medium studied Julia closely. "You appear relaxed, child. Are you in good health and clear mind? It is very important that you are sound in both mind and body because the trip may be extremely taxing for you."

"Trip?" Julia asked, knitting her brows slightly.

"You will journey far, if the spirits so permit," the medium said. "You will travel a long, long way. Your mind must be open to receive any and all messages from beyond that those of the other world desire to impart to you. You do believe?" the medium asked.

Julia felt confused and slightly embarrassed at being the focus of everyone's attention. She felt her mouth go dry. Her throat felt tight. She nodded, feeling that a nod would not be as grave a lie as a spoken word. She actually did not truly believe, yet she felt that some good might come out of the séance.

Everyone was smiling at her. There was a lovely feeling of belonging and she suddenly found herself relaxing in her chair. Whatever was in store for her, she felt she was among friends and nothing terrible would happen.

"We'll begin now," the medium said as she closed her eyes and tilted her head back. Almost immediately, as if the closing of her eyes had been a signal, the room went black. The blackness gradually turned into an eerie glow from the single bulb that hung suspended over the round table.

Julia felt the woman on her left take hold of her hand; the frail blond youth took her other hand, giving it a friendly squeeze. She saw the hands around the table touch, making a human chain. She felt a slight discomfort at sitting there with two complete strangers holding her hands. She had never been subjected to physical contact with others, except on extremely rare occasions, and the idea of hand-holding made her a trifle embarrassed.

The medium began chanting in Latin and Julia found herself forgetting her discomfort and her embarrassment and concentrated on what was about to transpire. She found herself being lulled into a deeper state of relaxation. The foreign words drifted softly over the group around the table. Julia had forgotten most of the Latin taught her, but found she could translate some of what the medium was chanting: "Great spirit of the universe, we conjure you up...." There followed a whole string of strange names, none of which Julia recognized. Then she heard a name she did recognize: "Beelzebub." She knew very well who that was and unconsciously found her hands tightening on the hands clasped in hers.

The chanting went on and on and on and Julia found she wasn't translating any more. The soft, soothing voice was gently lulling her into a wonderful state of restfulness. She felt a wonderful glow burning inside her and suddenly she felt weightless, as though she were no longer under the control of the earth's gravitational pull. She was floating. Her body was suspended in a void of unlimited expanse.

"Johavam, Tagla, Mathon, Oarios, Almouzin...."

A thick carpet of feathery down closed in on her. Her eyes were blinded by a sudden brilliance of color that spun and rocketed all around her. Pinwheels of flashing sparks twirled and spiralled; bursts of liquid gold splashed in every direction; fireballs of scalding red zoomed over, around and through her.

"Salmandrae, Gnomus, Godens, Gigua, Belial, Diabolus...."

The sound of a rushing wind all but deafened her. Her throat felt parched and clogged with dust.

"Come to us, O great and powerful Master of the Universe. Tell us what secrets are to be known about this humble subject. Tell us of Julia Carson."

Through her clouded vision Julia saw a tall, masculine shape materialize. The outline looked familiar. She felt she'd seen it before somewhere, but could not recall just where. Again she heard her name, but this time it was a man who called to her.

"Julia Carson. Julia. Come to me." The shadowy figure beckoned to her. "Come to me, not as you are now, but as you should be."

Julia found herself repeating the man's words. "Come as I should be."

The shadowy figure kept saying the same thing again and again. "Come not as you are now but as you should be. Come not as you are now but as you should be." His shape came closer and closer but Julia could not see the face, only the outline of broad shoulders, tall stature, trim body. The figure beckoned again and asked, "Will you come, Julia?"

Unconsciously, she found herself saying, "Yes, I will come."

Again the shadowy figure beckoned to her and Julia heard him say, "Remember. Come to me, but do not come as you are now, but as you should be." Then the figure began to dissolve and the boundaries of the void moved closer together until the void no longer existed.

Julia found herself standing high atop a rocky pinnacle. Below was what appeared to be a huge, majestic city. Lights blinked and twinkled like so many diamonds. A strong, cold wind threatened to topple her from her vantage point. The wind was blowing full in her face, taking her breath away. Its volume and force became steadily louder and stronger. Her hair streamed out behind her. Her body ached from the cold. She tried to wrap her arms about her in order to warm her bones but her arms were pinned to her sides. Then, at the height of the tumult, she saw a familiar face. The medium's face stared down at her from a dark, grey cloud. Their eyes met and held for what seemed an eternity. The medium pointed an accusing finger at Julia.

"Daughter of evil...evil...evil...evil...."

"No!" Julia yelled and then everything suddenly went blank. Julia could hear her own scream and gradually she heard the hurried murmur of voices all around her. She opened her eyes slowly, afraid of what she might see. She found herself seated at a round table. Her hands were clasped firmly in the hands of two complete strangers.

Julia shook herself and tried to smother the aching in her head. Tears were streaming from her eyes. Her body was bathed in sweat. People moved and began speaking more loudly, but she could not understand a thing. The only word she could hear was "Evil...Evil...Evil."

She felt something wet on her wrists and temples, and realized that someone was dabbing her with a cold, damp cloth. Fred

McAndrews touched her elbow and helped her rise from her chair. Her legs felt like gelatin. Every muscle in her body ached and throbbed in pain. She allowed herself to be led to a soft, overstuffed chair that sat near a heavily draped window. Fred McAndrews drew back the draperies and opened the window slightly. The cold, damp sea air swept over her and wiped away the cobwebs. Julia felt her strength gradually return, along with her sanity.

"Julia. Julia," the medium said softly.

Slowly Julia turned her eyes on the strange little woman. "You knew my name all along," Julia found herself saying.

The medium did not seem to sense Julia's anger. "No, my dear. Your name was given me by the powers from beyond." The medium reached out to smooth Julia's hair. Julia pulled back sharply. "Tell us, child, what you saw? Was anything told to you?"

Julia spoke but she did not recognize her own voice. It was as if someone else was speaking through her mouth. "You know very well what was said to me," she said angrily.

"But I do not," the medium insisted.

"You do. You were there," Julia said, feeling her anger building and building. "I saw you!"

The little woman backed away. "Me? I don't understand," the medium said, staring with dismay at Julia's angry face.

Julia's anger burst forth full force. "You understand perfectly well. You called me evil...'daughter of evil.' How dare you say such a thing of me? You don't know me."

Fred McAndrews took her in his arms. "There, there, Julia. Control yourself. My aunt is not responsible for the things she says or does when she slips into her catatonic state. She remembers nothing. Please calm yourself. Try to understand and remember what happened to you back there."

"She said I was the daughter of evil," Julia cried, and then collapsed against Fred McAndrews' shoulder in a burst of tears.

His arm went about her. He patted her shoulder. "I'm sure it means nothing. Calm yourself." He heard his aunt gasp. When he looked at her, he saw her face grow pale. She was standing rigid, as though frozen. Her eyes stared straight ahead. "I remember," she droned. "I remember a man appearing to me. He had been speaking with Julia, asking her to come to him. Julia agreed. The man turned to me and told me to prepare her for what she must do."

Gradually what the medium was saying began to filter into Julia's consciousness. She turned on the woman. "Prepare me for what?" Julia demanded, trying to control her sobbing.

"I do not know that. All I know is that I was told to send you back to your past so that you might begin again."

"Begin again?"

The medium shook her head. "It is all slipping away from me again," she said. "All I know is that you must begin where you started; that is what he told me to tell you."

"He? Who?"

"That I do not know. He said you must begin where you started and from there your way will be clear. Somewhere back in the beginning a wrong course was taken. You must go back and find the right one."

"Go back? Go back where?" Julia asked.

The medium looked vague. "To the beginning," she answered. "That is all I know to tell you."

Julia found her anger had subsided completely. "But you said I was the daughter of evil. What did you mean? Did he tell you to call me that?"

"What it means is a mystery to me, my child. I do know that you must go back to your beginning. Perhaps the answers will be made known to you there." The medium reached out and took Julia's hand. "I am not trying to frighten you, Julia. I saw something strange in your past. What I referred to when I called you 'daughter of evil' I do not know. However, I sense that there was a great wrong done many, many years ago and you must go back and right that wrong, whatever it was."

"You aren't making any sense. I know of no terrible wrong I did."

"I did not say the wrong was done by you, Julia. Perhaps the key word in your strange experience was 'daughter.' Perhaps it was a wrong of your parents which you must make right."

"I have no parents. I was a foundling."

The medium's eyes brightened. "Then there is where you must begin. That is what it all means. Yes, yes, I see now. You must find yourself...your true self. You are not Julia Carson but another girl. Go, look to your past and rid yourself of the accusations that seem to be clinging to you...following you." The medium leaned closer and peered deep into Julia's eyes.

"Who are you, my child?" the medium asked. "Who are you really? Find the answer to that question, Julia. Go. Find the answer."

CHAPTER SIX

Julia took her leave of Elizabeth, Allyson, and Margaret with dry eyes. Naturally, the girls were surprised that Julia decided to return to the city after just two days of vacation, but no one tried to persuade her to stay.

"If Julia wants to waste the money deposited on the hotel room, well, that's her business," Margaret had said.

They tried, of course, to uncover the "real" reason Julia was cutting her vacation short. They were convinced it had something to do with the date she'd kept the previous night.

"She's most likely going off with some man," Margaret had said.

Elizabeth had admonished her slightly, but only slightly. In the back of her mind Elizabeth believed Margaret could well be right.

She was glad none of the girls offered to come to the station with her. If they had, they would have learned that Julia had no intention whatever of taking the train back to the city. Instead, she purchased a ticket for a city in a neighboring state. From there she changed trains twice, finally arriving at a sleepy little village. The sign over the prim train depot read ROSSMORE.

The last time Julia remembered seeing that sign was two years ago, when she boarded this very train which ultimately led her to New York. She never thought she'd be returning here of her own free will. She never thought she would want to see Rossmore again. The town held a lot of unpleasant memories, and each and every one of them was etched deeply in her mind.

"Why, Miss Julie," the old stationmaster said as she stepped down from the train. "Lordy, I never expected to see you back in this here town again."

Julia gave him a big smile. Mr. Petticord had been the only person in Rossmore who ever showed any signs of friendliness. He was a gristled old codger, but for some reason he'd taken a liking to the scrawny little girl who used to run away from the orphanage and hide in the freight office, intent upon stowing away on the first train headed out of town. Each time he'd find her and manage to talk her into waiting until she was older before facing all the terrible things that lay in wait for her outside Rossmore. Each time he would tell of a different horror, a horror suited to her age of understanding, and each time she'd relent and allow him to take her back to the orphanage where, he would tell her, she at least had a roof over her head and was given regular, although sometimes inadequate, meals. There were many, many times, however, when Julia would have rather starved and slept in an open field than face the cruelties and hardships the people at the orphanage levied on her.

"Mr. Petticord," Julia said, giving him a quick hug. The old man returned the embrace in that strained, reluctant, slightly embarrassed manner of his. It was the only form of affection Julia had ever received.

"You shouldn't be bringing yourself back here, Miss Julie. It took you too long to get away from the likes of a place like this."

"I know," Julia said, "but there's something I must find out. It's awfully important."

"It must be, to bring you back. What must you find out?"

"Fix me one of your delicious cups of tea and I'll tell you all about myself," Julia said as she herded him into the train office.

The old man glanced up and down the platform. The train was pulling out, the station was empty of passengers.

No one came to Rossmore, except when one of the matrons went to fetch a waif. The only regular business the train station saw was those trying to run away or those old enough to leave with the orphanage's begrudged permission.

As Mr. Petticord fussed with the tea, Julia told him all that had happened to her since leaving Rossmore, but she did not tell all of the details of the last few days. During her formative years she had learned how to shade the truth in order to escape punishment and she utilized that faculty now. Once, long ago, Mr. Petticord had warned her about fortune-telling gypsys and mystics who believed in spirits and ghosts and such. So she told Mr. Petticord about having met someone who seemed to know her. In Julia's mind this had been the old gypsy woman. This person who seemed to recognize her said she was not Julia Carson, but someone else. Julia purposely omitted all mention of the séance and the terrible accusations made of her.

"So I've got to get into the office of the orphanage and have a look at my records. Surely they must have some information as to where I came from."

"But Miss Julie. You know sure as shootin' that old Miss Marshall ain't going to just let you walk in and go through her records."

"Oh, I realize that, Mr. Petticord. I also know that Miss Marshall and the rest of the staff go to bed about ten-thirty every night. The place is locked but I know how to get in." Julia paused and thought for a moment. "If I had suspected then that I was not Julia Carson, there would have been no need for me to be back here now. Of course, I'd always been tempted to look up my records just to see if there was any mention of my parents' whereabouts, but the penalties for that were pretty severe, and I had always been a coward when it came to taking punishment."

Mr. Petticord shook his head. "The penalties will be much more severe if you get yourself caught now. They'll charge you with breaking and entering. That's a criminal offense, Miss Julie. I'd not suggest you take the chance."

"But I must, Mr. Petticord. Don't you see? Put yourself in my place. Suppose someone told you they knew for sure that your name was not Petticord. Wouldn't you try everything within your power to find out who you really are?"

Old Mr. Petticord rubbed his chin. "Well, I suppose it would be tempting, Miss Julie, but couldn't the authorities help you get to the bottom of this?"

"What authorities? Once a child is given to an orphanage, her true origin is obliterated. The child is never told who its real parents are or were. Oh, I know I'll be committing a crime by breaking into the orphanage's records, but I can't help myself. I must do it, Mr. Petticord. I must."

Mr. Petticord said nothing. Deep down inside he knew he'd want to do the same thing if he were in Julia's situation, but he remained quiet; he didn't want to encourage her. He knew that if they caught her, Julia Carson would never stand a chance of exoneration. The orphanage ruled Rossmore. The chief of police was the matron's brother. The judge of the town was the brother of the chief of police. It was a closely knit community, and Julia would not be able to stand up to it if she got caught.

Mr. Petticord knew of all the cruelties perpetrated in the name of human kindness. The state inspectors that showed up once every several years were shown only what Miss Marshall and her fiendish cohorts wanted them to see. The children were mistreated, overworked, and underfed. No one ever knew why Mr. Petticord stayed on as stationmaster, knowing what he knew. He would never tell what he knew because he'd made that mistake once and had been paying for it ever since.

"Please, Miss Julie. Try to forget about what someone told you about yourself. Leave Rossmore before someone from the orphanage sees you. They'll assume you're up to no good 'cause that's the way they all think." He leaned across the little table and took her hand. His grip was stronger than she'd expected it to be. "You must leave here, Miss Julie. It'll mean trouble for you if you try to do what you're planning."

Julia saw fear in the old man's eyes, yet there was a strange power inside her urging her on. "No, I must find out what I can about myself, Mr. Petticord. Regardless of the consequences, I must do what I've come to do."

The old man shook his head. "You're making a terrible mistake, Miss Julie. A terrible mistake. They'll catch you for sure."

"Please don't worry yourself about me, Mr. Petticord. I'll be careful. I promise."

"You'll have to be more than just careful. You've got to be lucky. Them folks are all like hawks when it comes to searching out people to make trouble for. I'm warning you, Miss Julie. I won't be able to raise a finger to help if you get yourself into a mess."

Julia patted his hand. She had always been aware of Mr. Petticord's fear of the people who ran the orphanage and Rossmore, but she never knew the root of that fear. Whatever it was, was Mr. Petticord's secret, and he obviously had no intention of divulging it to anyone.

"I understand, Mr. Petticord. I'll not implicate you in any way. But please don't worry about me. I'll not get into trouble. I know a way onto the grounds that will prove safe enough, and I know how to get into the main building through a cellar door with a loose hinge. Knowing how miserly Miss Marshall is about spending for repairs, I'm sure no one's fixed the hinge. I'll wait until it's very dark. The watchman makes his rounds on the quarter hour. I'll time it just right, so you have nothing to worry about."

Mr. Petticord shook his head. "Anybody that ventures anywhere near that old, hellish place has something to worry about, Miss Julie. But I suppose no one wants to listen to the warnings of an old man. You'll do what you've come to do, and no one will be able to sway you from that, I can see that by the look in your eye."

Julia smiled at him. "No, no one can persuade me to do other than what I've come to do. I must find out about myself. It never seemed really important before, but now...well, now it's the most important thing in the world to me. There seems to be something inside driving me on."

Mr. Petticord slapped his legs and let out a sigh. "Well," he said, pushing himself up out of the chair, "I suppose you should be getting some rest if you intend traipsing around all night.

I'll make up the cot in the other room. You'll be safe enough there. Nobody comes around to the depot this time of day." He started away but at the doorway he stopped and turned back. "Are you hungry, Miss Julie? I could easily enough fix you up some grub."

Julia shook her head. "I'm too keyed up to eat. Thank you anyway, Mr. Petticord. I'll just lie down until nightfall. Maybe some rest will improve my appetite."

But when Julia awoke, her appetite had not returned and the night was black as pitch. She opened her suitcase and took out her hairbrush and comb. She splashed cold water on her face and tidied herself as best she could. Mr. Petticord was sitting in front of a pot-bellied stove, puffing on a pipe. When Julia came into the cozy little room, he looked up from his reverie.

"You always were the prettiest little girl I ever did see," he said with a smile. He got to his feet. "I've fixed you some sandwiches in case you were hungry."

She thanked him and forced herself to nibble on one of them. "What time is it?" she asked.

"Oh, long about eleven or so," he told her.

"I should get started then," she said. "Will you keep an eye on my bags until I get back?"

"I'll put them in the freight office with the rest of the freight. If anyone comes nosing around, they'll think they're just some things waiting to be shipped out."

"It'll take me about half an hour to walk to the orphanage," Julia said more to herself than to the old man. "I'd best get started. Everyone should have turned in by now so chances are I'll not be seen."

"Don't take any chances, Miss Julie. Go by the back way. It might be a little longer, but it'll prove safer in the long run, I think."

Julia agreed. She slipped the uneaten portion of the sandwich back into the wax paper Mr. Petticord had wrapped it in and tucked it into her handbag. "I should be back here around one or one-thirty if all goes well," she told him.

"God be with you, child," he said. He spoke in a whisper as he opened the door for her. He spoke as if there were waiting ears standing just outside.

Julia paused, looking around to get her bearings. Heavy clouds made the night darker and colder than usual. She tugged her light coat tightly around her shoulders, and hurried away from the lighted windows of the train station, stepping into darkness.

She went along the road that led eventually to the town itself, but before walking a quarter of a mile, she veered off onto a path barely twenty-inches wide and well overgrown with tall grass and scraggly little weeds that threatened to trip her. She made her way along the dark and lonely little path for more than a mile, feeling all the while that there was someone watching her. More than once she turned and looked back over her shoulder to make absolutely certain she was alone on this moonless night. Each time she turned she saw nothing, yet the moment she started up again she felt convinced that there was someone walking directly behind her...following her. Strangely enough, she had the feeling that whoever was shadowing her meant her no harm. It was as if a guiding force was pushing her on to her destination.

The path sloped down toward a narrower, almost nonexistent path. It was no more than an animal run, hardly ever used by humans. She trudged along, being careful where she put her feet, for she knew the holes and rocks and pitfalls the uneven ground offered. She walked until her legs began to ache. Then the path opened up and she found herself in a wide field of tall grass. The earth beneath her feet turned marshy and she went more slowly than before.

Julia did not see the orphanage wall until she was almost upon it. She'd approached from the left of the main gate. Quickly she skirted the wall and went around to the rear where the little graveyard lay with its untended sod and toppling grave markers. She used to spend a lot of time here in this tiny cemetery, memorizing the names of the dead babies. She had always thought of them as her friends. How many times had she sat there, crying, wishing she too lay with them?

She had little time for tears or memories now, she told herself as she went quickly past the gravestones. She went toward the wall and felt along with her hands until she found what she was searching for. A thick, thorny vine stretched up over the top of the wall and beneath the thorny vine was her secret passage, which was nothing more than a hidden fissure wide enough to crawl through. As a child, she had had no trouble squeezing through the crack. Now, however, it was a different story. She found, surprisingly enough, that her dimensions hadn't changed all that much since she last ventured this way. She'd forgotten, however, how sharp and prickly the thorns were and came through the passage with quite a few scratches, some of which had drawn blood.

She couldn't think about that now, she told herself as she stood against the wall staring at the barred windows of the orphanage. In her mind she clicked off the rooms to which the windows belonged. Kitchen, dining hall, storage room, she said, counting the windows from right to left. She headed toward the windows of the storage room and from there, went around the corner of the building, crouching low in case someone might be watching. All the windows were dark, luckily—all except the light in the night watchman's room, which she saw at the far end of the building.

She came to the cellar doors leading down into the fruit bins. She ran her hand along the edge until she found the broken hinge. Carefully she examined it to make sure it hadn't been repaired. Luck was with her. Being mindful not to make a sound, she raised up the corner of the door as far as the other hinge would permit it to be elevated. She fitted herself under the levered door and slipped onto the steps that led downward.

Once she lowered the door into its proper place, she wondered idly if it were possible to step from black to blacker. The fruit cellar was the color of pitch and as dismal as the graveyard beyond the wall. It had a pleasant enough aroma, but that was the only thing pleasant about the place. Cobwebs hung in profusion from every beam and corner. The slab floor was thick with gray, spongy dust that made Julia's steps soundless.

She groped around the wall, feeling her way. It had been a while since she'd last been in the fruit cellar, but she remembered the last time most vividly. It wasn't a pleasant memory and she brushed it quickly from her mind.

Slowly, carefully, she made her way past the shelves, lockers, and bins toward where she reckoned the door sat in the wall. After what seemed an eternity, her fingers finally felt the square door panels. The wood felt moldy, rough, and unfriendly. She searched for the knob. Her hand tightened around the porcelain knob. She twisted it slowly, not wanting to make a sound. She exerted a steady, even pressure. The knob seemed rusted fast. She turned it harder. She used all of her strength. She felt a kind of panic beginning to creep up inside her throat as she realized that the latch wasn't rusted. The door was locked. She fumbled for the key beneath the knob, knowing it would not be there. She turned the knob harder, hoping to break the lock. She suddenly didn't care if they heard her or not. Memories of having been locked in the fruit cellar were bringing back an old panic. She felt that she was going to scream.

Then, to add to her terrifying fear, she heard a voice.

"Who's there?" someone demanded.

CHAPTER SEVEN

Julia felt her blood turn to ice. She pressed herself hard against the door, unable to breathe, unable to think. She was trapped. This was the end. She was finished, she thought

"Who are you? Who's there?" the voice asked again.

Something in its tone told Julia it *was* a child asking.

"It's Julie...Julie Carson," she ventured, thinking she recognized the familiar voice of one of the children she'd been responsible for at one time. She strained to see through the dark. "Is that you, Meg?" She looked in the direction from which she thought the little voice had come. "Where are you?"

"Oh, Julie. Yes, it's me, Meg. I'm over here by the stack of apple baskets."

Julia found little Meg cowering against a stack of empty baskets which were used in the fall to collect the apples from the trees in the south orchard.

"Meg, honey. Why are you being disciplined?"

The fruit cellar was a favorite place for establishing discipline. Meg was not the first, nor would she be the last, frightened child to be locked up for the night in order to meditate about how bad she'd been. It was often difficult for the children to reflect on their badness when nothing bad had been done by them. But those in authority thought otherwise, and cared little about the terrible consequences a child might suffer from a terrifying night of being locked in a black hole without hope of release.

"I dropped my dinner tray and spilled everything all over the floor," the little girl sobbed. "Oh, Julie, did you come back to take me with you?"

Julia felt for the girl and the moment she touched her, Meg leaped from where she cowered and flung herself against Julia, wrapping her arms tightly around Julia's neck. The frightened child broke into uncontrollable crying.

"There, there, little Meg. Everything is going to be all right."

"I'm so afraid," the girl sobbed. "Take me away, Julie. Take me away from here. I want to go away with you."

How desperately Julia wished she could take little Meg out of the terrible place. How she wished she could take all of them away. Too vividly she remembered her own childhood with its thrashings, the work punishments, the nights without dinner, the solitary confinements. She had been no bigger than Meg when she was first thrust into this horrible cellar and left to the terrors only a small child's mind is susceptible to. Time, of course, hardened her to the evils of the place. She became indifferent to the sadistic treatment, as Meg someday would. She learned to endure and to bide her time until she was old enough to be sent out on her own. And the only reason they ever allowed any of the girls to leave the orphanage was because the state did not pay for the orphan's maintenance after age eighteen.

Yes, Julia thought as she cradled the crying child in her arms, little Meg would grow hard and bitter and callous. She would have to or she would never survive. Poor Meg wasn't pretty enough for anyone to want to adopt her.

Julia heard footsteps outside the door—the night watchman making his rounds. She would have to get out of her predicament somehow. She couldn't bring herself to go back; that would accomplish nothing. Perhaps she should return tomorrow on the chance that the fruit-cellar door would be unlocked. But chances were she'd be seen and reported and they'd make trouble. No, time was of the essence. She was inside the orphanage now and she felt she had to make the best of it.

Julia eased little Meg away. "Stop crying now, darling, and let me see if I can't get us out of here," she said.

The child allowed Julia to put her aside. She sat back against the baskets, wrapping her arms around her knees, and laid her face on her arms. She sat there in the dark listening to Julia fumbling with the door latch.

"I can't see the hall light through the keyhole," Julia said, "so the key must be still in the lock on the other side." She sat there thinking for a moment, then snatched up her handbag and pulled out the half-eaten sandwich Mr. Petticord had made for her. "Are you hungry, Meg?" she asked.

"Oh, yes," the little girl said.

Julia fitted the sandwich into the child's hands. She took the wax paper in which it had been wrapped and flattened it out. Carefully she fitted it under the bottom edge of the door, directly beneath the latch. She searched in her purse for a pencil. Using the eraser end as a battering ram she jabbed the pencil into the keyhole and butted it up against the key that was lodged there. It took a few minutes to work the key loose but after several attempts, Julia heard the heavy key drop with a soft clang onto the wax paper. Carefully she withdrew the paper from under the door.

The key came with it.

With a thankful sigh she fitted the key into the latch and turned it as slowly and as quietly as she could. The rusty lock balked at first, but then the key turned and the lock clicked open. Julia let herself relax for a moment. She could feel the perspiration on her forehead and the dampness in her palms.

She sat quite still for a second or two, gathering her wits about her. If she'd heard the watchman at this end of the building, she figured, then he was just finishing his rounds and heading back to his quarters. She'd have to act fast.

But what was she to do about Meg? It would be impossible to take her away, yet it would be equally impossible to lock the child up again inside the dark, damp cellar. Julia bit down on her lower lip and tried to think.

"Meg," she said finally, "I'm going to open the door. There is a little light in the hall that will dispel the darkness. Will you be a real good girl and sit here with the door ajar and wait for me to come back for you?"

"Where are you going?" Meg asked, finishing off the sandwich.

"I have something I must find," Julia told her. "It's in Miss Marshall's office."

"Oh, but you mustn't go in there," Meg said. "They'll lock you up in that other terrible place and they won't feed you for days and days."

"I know, darling, I know," Julia said, embracing the child. "But I must take that chance. It is very, very important." She smoothed the child's hair. "Will you wait here for Julia? When I come back we'll figure out some way of getting you out of here."

"You'll take me with you?"

"We'll see, sweetheart, we'll see," Julia said, feeling sick at heart for having to encourage the child.

"I'll wait, Julie. I'll wait," Meg said happily, as she hugged Julia.

Julia swallowed the lump that caught in her throat. She eased the child away and turned the knob. The door opened with a creak. The light from the hall was dim and yellow but, nevertheless, it was light; it cut a dull streak across the cellar floor.

"Now, you sit here in the light, honey," she said. "Julia won't be very long."

"All right, Julie."

Quietly Julia slipped off her shoes and went out into the hall, shoes in hand. She strained to pick up any possible sound. She heard nothing but her own heart beating wildly in her breast. She pressed herself close against the wall and went down the corridor. At the end she glanced back. Meg was sitting with her anxious little face peering out at Julia through the crack in the door. Julia held up crossed fingers and stepped around the corner. A long stairway led upward, at the top of which was Miss Marshall's private office, next to which was the record office where she must begin her search.

As she climbed the stairs, being careful to put her feet at the side of the step closest to the wall, she again felt that someone was directly behind her, following in her footsteps. She thought for a moment that it might be little Meg, but when she turned she saw nothing...nothing at all. She tried to push the feeling out of her mind, but the sensation of being shadowed persisted.

She made her way to the door of the records office. She remembered that there was a burglar-alarm mechanism attached to its door. It was an invisible beam of light that passed across the threshold about twenty-four inches from the floor. She glanced down at the tiny beam glinting dully, which meant that the mechanism was in operation.

Julia pushed the door inward and eased her shoes and purse under the alarm beam. Then she lay flat on her stomach and—keeping her head low—crawled beneath the beam into the office. She made her way quickly toward the row upon row of file cabinets, but in the darkness of the room she could see none of the labels.

Hurriedly she went back to where her handbag lay and rummaged inside it for a possible book of matches. Her hands were shaking and she almost spilled the entire contents of her bag onto the floor in her anxiety to find something to provide her with light. She had no matches, no cigarette lighter, nothing to illuminate the labels. She stood there trying to figure out what to do. Her eyes traveled toward the door that connected the record office with Miss Marshall's private office. Miss Marshall smoked cigarettes, Julia remembered.

Quickly she went into the private office and began rummaging through the top drawer of the mahogany desk. She felt around until her fingers touched upon a half-empty pack of cigarettes. Next to it was a lighter.

The first cabinet she came to was marked CURRENT. Beside it was row upon row of cabinets arranged according to the letters of the alphabet. Just in case they hadn't gotten around to trans-ferring her records from the current files, Julia checked the "C" drawer but found no file for Julia Carson.

Across the room, arranged under the windows, was another

row of files. Julia saw the tag reading CLOSED. The night outside faintly illuminated the room, and being careful of not having the flame of the lighter seen by an alert pair of eyes from outside, she clicked out the lighter and strained to read the names in the drawer marked "C."

"Mia Carson," she whispered as she hurriedly pulled her file from its place. Her heart was beating faster. She carried the file away from the windows to a table in the center of the room. With unsteady hands she flipped it open. There were sheets and sheets of departmental records, maintenance figures, school grades, work data. She riffled through the papers. The flame from the lighter was faltering, growing smaller and dimmer. She read through the file papers as hurriedly as she could but found nothing but useless information. *The* very last paper at the bottom of the file was half the size of the other papers. It was almost missed by her as she finished flipping through the sheets. Luckily she noticed it before closing the file.

She held the flame closer to the paper. It was nothing more than a large-size index card. One glance told her it was what she was searching for. She saw her name printed in bold black letters at the top. Beneath her name there was a space marked "Date of Admittance" which was filled in with a date.

The flame from the lighter spat and flickered and threatened to snuff itself out.

Julia ripped the card out of the file. She was sure this was what she had come to find.

The cigarette lighter refused to work. She'd have to chance the desk light in Miss Marshall's office, she decided. But her decision was thwarted by an unexpected calamity.

The burglar alarm went off.

CHAPTER EIGHT

Julia heard a scream which she thought was her own, just as the alarm system blasted out its ear-shattering clanging. Lights flashed on and the place seemed to come alive with noise and motion. She stared at the open door of the record office. The scream she had heard had come from the doorway and standing there, eyes wide with fright, was Meg. Frightened into blind flight, Meg turned and rushed back down the hallway. Julia started after her, but when she heard the voices of Miss Marshall and the others, she froze in her tracks. Her shoes and bag were lying just inside the door. She snatched them up and hid herself behind a row of filing cabinets.

She heard Meg squeal and—as much as she wanted to—Julia forced herself not to interfere.

"How did you get out of the cellar?" she heard one of the women yell.

"The door's open," a man said—an old man's voice; the night watchman, no doubt, Julia decided.

"I locked it myself," the woman said.

"You most likely forgot, Martha." It was Miss Marshall's imperious voice. "You forgot to turn the key in the lock once before. Remember?" she added icily.

"What was she doing upstairs?" Julia heard the matron ask.

"Most likely just wandered around and got herself lost," the night watchman said.

Miss Marshall boomed, "Will someone please turn off that blasted alarm. It's breaking my eardrums."

Julia heard footsteps coming all the way up the stairs. They crossed the hall. A switch was obviously thrown somewhere because the alarm went dead and the lights blinked out. She listened, waiting to hear footsteps coming into the records office to investigate, but she heard only the footsteps of someone going back down the hall and down the stairs. She heaved a sigh of relief and sagged against one of the cabinets.

She heard poor little Meg crying hysterically. Julia tried not to think of the punishment that lay in store for the child. Extra work, quarter rations, solitary confinement. Julia remembered it all only too plainly, and she could not keep back the tears that welled up in her eyes. If only she could do something. What? What would be gained by trying to rescue Meg? They'd only throw trouble her way as well.

The voices kept on for a short while. She heard the night watchman again mounting the stairs and checking the rooms. Luckily she was not discovered. She stayed huddled in the corner of the record office and waited until she felt it was safe to make her escape.

After a long while she took a deep breath and screwed up her courage. She stepped out of her hiding place and headed for the door, clutching her shoes and her bag tight against her body. Again she had to open the door of the record room, this time from the inside, as the night watchman had pulled it closed when he reset the alarm. The beam, fortunately, did not control the opening or closing of the door, only the traffic that passed through it. She saw the little alarm light blinking at her. She repeated her earlier actions, this time in reverse.

Silent as a cat she crept down the stairs. Everything was as still and as quiet as purple velvet. The lower floor was empty. She rounded the corner of the hall and headed for the door to the fruit cellar. She half expected it to be closed and locked and was wondering what she would do about Meg, when to her surprise she saw the door was standing open. They obviously changed their minds about confining Meg back in the cellar. She wondered if they had a more terrifying cell of confinement which they now used.

But she mustn't think about Meg and her problems; she had problems of her own, she reminded herself. Quickly she went into the fruit cellar, slipped on her shoes and made her way up through the cellar door with the broken hinge. She hurried across the grounds until she found the crack in the wall. She retraced her steps back through the tiny graveyard, the open field and the overgrown path.

Once out of sight of the orphanage, she rested against a tree and tried to get her breathing back to normal. She slipped her hand in her purse and pulled out the record card she'd taken. There was no moon and the card was but a blur. The printing on it was totally illegible in the darkness of the night. She pushed it back into her handbag and found she had also taken Miss Marshall's cigarette lighter.

She stiffened and turned sharply when she heard someone say, "Thief."

Her eyes were wide, her mouth open. A scream lay ready in her throat. She saw no one. The wood was empty. Only trees and shrubs and the tall grass kept her company. Yet she was certain she'd heard a man speak. She strained, looking hard into the darkness. She heard no one—no sound at all but that of her own heavy breathing.

Julie pushed herself away from the tree and started back toward the train depot and safety. As she walked along, again she felt the strange yet familiar presence directly behind her. However, whenever she turned to check, she found nothing there.

Yes, she was a thief, and the thought suddenly bothered her more than she cared to admit.

Yet, strangely enough, there was a pulsing in her temples that kept telling her that there had been nothing wrong in what she'd done.

She shook her head. She thought back over the last few days. She couldn't understand why she'd been compelled to do what she did. It was as if she had acted under the power of someone else. It hadn't been the timid, reserved Julie Carson who stole into that office and pilfered the files.

Just as the town clock struck the one-thirty bell, she tapped on the railway stationmaster's door.

"Miss Julie, child. My you're a sight for sore eyes," Mr. Petticord said. "I see you made it, all right."

"Not without incident," Julia said as she entered the cozy little room.

"What happened?"

Julia told him as quickly as she could.

Mr. Petticord shook his head. "Poor little girl. You say you knew her?"

"Yes, she was just a tiny thing but she remembered me. Oh, Mr. Petticord, I just can't stop thinking about what they'll do to that poor baby."

"Now, now. You've survived their hellish treatments; this little Meg will survive it, too. Don't think about it anymore, Miss Julie. Put it out of your head. There's nothing that can be done now."

Julia sighed. "I suppose you're right," she said resignedly.

Mr. Petticord brightened. "And you think you found what you went after?" he asked anxiously.

Julia roused herself. "Yes," she said, slipping the record card from her bag. "I haven't had a chance to read it yet. There wasn't time inside the orphanage and there wasn't any moon or light to see by once I got outside."

"Well, look at it, girl," Mr. Petticord urged. "Look at it. What does it tell you?"

Julia scanned the card. Again she saw her name, "JULIA CARSON," printed in big letters at the top. Again she saw the blank filled in under "Date of Admittance." The next line held what she needed to know: "Name of Parents: BRIDGET BISHOP (FATHER UNKNOWN)."

"My name is Bishop," she said, feeling a strange tingling running through her. She stared at the name and felt like shouting it out loud. "Bishop," she repeated happily.

"That was your mother's name," Mr. Petticord reminded her. "It says there that your father was unknown," he added as he read over her shoulder.

Of course, Julia thought. He's right. My father's name might well have been anything...Carson, even. The medium and the fortune teller might still be wrong in saying my name is not Julia Carson.

She looked back at the card.

"Place of birth: BELHAM, MASS."

Julia frowned. "Belham, Massachusetts? I've never heard of it," she told Mr. Petticord.

He rubbed his chin and cocked his head to one side. "Can't say I have either." Then he snapped his fingers. "But we can sure find out quick enough. I have the train listings for every city and town in the country. If there ain't no railroad into that place Belham, then the book'll tell you which is the nearest station. I'll go check." He hurried toward the office and was back with a thick, dogeared tome which he flipped open and started scanning the listings. "Massachusetts...Here we are," he said. "Belham, Belham.... Yep, Belham. It's near Salem," he added, running his finger across the page. "Must be a tiny little place 'cause there ain't no trains go anywhere near there. You change trains at Salem to a town called Peabody. From Peabody you gotta take a bus or shuttle into Weaver, which is a pretty good piece northeast of there, and Belham is just a hop, skip, and a jump from Weaver, but there ain't no signs of a bus or anything going into Belham."

"Massachusetts." Julia said. She felt a warm glow around her heart. "At least I know now where I came from. You have no idea how wonderful it is to know that you have a home state and a home town."

Mr. Petticord was going to remark that a hometown was a place where one was born and raised, but he thought better of it.

"What time can I get a train out of here?" Julia asked, suddenly restless and anxious to get started.

"There's one at seven-thirty in the morning. It'll take you to the capital where you can change trains. I'll get busy and write you up a ticket." He started toward the ticket cage, but hesitated and turned back. "It would be a lot quicker for you to fly," he said, but he had a questioning look on his face.

"Fly? I've never been on an airplane in my life. I'd be frightened to death. The train will do very well, even if it is a bit slower."

"You have old-fashioned thinking, Miss Julie," he said brightly. A broad grin spread across his face. "I guess that's why I like you as much as I do."

"Thank you, Mr. Petticord. You're a very wonderful man and I will never forget you."

Mr. Petticord cleared his throat and looked embarrassed. "You'd better get yourself into bed. Get some sleep. I'll get you up in plenty of time to make the train."

Julia was tempted to admit she was hungry, but she didn't want to take time for food. Having been raised to know what hunger felt like, she did not mind sleeping on an empty stomach. She was used to it.

Soon she would be on her way home, she told herself as she went into the little room next to the depot office. "Belham," she said. "Bridget Bishop. Belham, Massachusetts." It all had a nice, strong ring to it, she decided. Father unknown. Of course, it was possible that her name really was Bishop. Bishop could well have been her father's name, her mother's married name. She sat up in bed, realizing that she had not examined the rest of the card.

The remaining portion of the front of the card had been blank, she remembered, but she'd forgotten to look on the back of the card. More information might be printed on the reverse side.

She got the card out of her purse and flipped it over. There were several blocks that were empty of information. At the very bottom of the card one single blank was filled in: "Reason for orphanage: MOTHER DECEASED."

Julia stared at the words. "Mother deceased," she said, letting her hand drop into her lap. Had all her efforts been for nothing?

She had found out where she came from only to discover that her father was unknown and her mother was dead. What good would it do her to go on to Belham now? She would only find a dead end when she got there.

Or perhaps her father was still living. Perhaps there was someone in Belham who knew Bridget Bishop and who knew who Bridget Bishop had married, or who had sired her child.

Wearily Julia crawled back into bed. She had lain down earlier with a much lighter heart. She had thought her journey would end at Belham, but now she realized that Belham might be only the beginning of a long and tedious search.

CHAPTER NINE

Julia thought she would not have slept well, but she was out like a light until Mr. Petticord tapped on the door and awakened her to the heavenly smell of breakfast cooking. The day was glorious, she noticed as she looked out at the sunlit landscape. The serenity of the deserted railroad yard, the tall, swaying pepper trees and the birds chirping gaily seemed to be omens of the happy future that she knew was waiting for her. She luxuriated in the peace and tranquility that embraced her. The dark days lay behind; from now on all her tomorrows would be as bright and as glorious as right now, she thought.

Her beautiful mood almost slipped away from her when thoughts of Meg and the dreary orphanage began to plague her. She reminded herself quickly that she had survived the terrible ordeal of growing up in that orphanage and if she had survived, Meg would survive.

She felt sad saying good-bye to Mr. Petticord. She would never return to Rossmore; both of them knew that. She would never see the old man who had been so kind and helpful. She kissed his cheek. She was bidding farewell forever to everything in her old life. All her lonely years were finished. She'd never go back to her furnished room in New York; there was nothing there she really needed or wanted. She'd never go to that chrome-and-glass office. She'd never venture anywhere near anything that might remind her of her old existence—her life as Julia Carson. Julia Carson ceased to exist.

Julia saw old Mr. Petticord blink back the tears that glistened in his eyes. "I ain't crying 'cause you're leaving here, Miss Julie," he said, wiping the back of his hand across his eyes. "These here are tears of happiness for you."

The train gave a warning blast of its whistle.

"Now, you get yourself out of here and I don't want to see you around this place again, hear?"

Not finding anything to say, Julia kissed his cheek again and got on board. She turned at the top of the metal steps and waved. The train gave a lurch and she grabbed the handrail for support. The wheels began to turn. The train moved forward, slowly at first, but gradually increasing its speed. Julia stood, leaning out, waving at Mr. Petticord until he and Rossmore were nothing more than names in her past.

Mr. Petticord's railroad schedule proved to be very out of date, Julia found. It was necessary for her to change twice before arriving at the Salem station. At Salem she made a convenient connection to Peabody, but at Peabody she was told there weren't any such places as Weaver or Belham.

"Of course there are," Julia insisted. "There must be. I was born in Belham," she told the young station agent. She felt her heart swell with pride.

He scratched the top of his head. "Well, I never heard of either of them," he admitted. He shook his head slowly and turned to an older man who was bent over a ticket desk. "Hey, Bill. Ever hear of any towns around these parts called Weaver and Belham?"

"Heard of Weaver," the man named Bill said. "Not sure I ever heard of Belham though." He thought for a moment. "Wait a minute. Now that I come to think of it, Belham *is* up near Weaver. Check the map, Andy."

The younger agent pulled out a large map and began scanning it. "I don't see any town called Belham listed." His finger moved down the listings. "Here's Weaver, though. M-5." He leaned closer over the map. "Yeah, here's Weaver all right." He scratched his head again. "Funny, I never heard of that town before." He looked up at Julia who was waiting patiently. "Are you sure the town you're looking for is Belham?"

"Yes. B-e-l-h-a-m."

He shook his head. "No such place. Here, see for yourself." He turned the map around so Julia could see the index.

She ran her eyes down the B's. He was right. No town of Belham was listed. "But the other gentleman said Belham was near Weaver."

"Hey, Bill. Are you sure about Belham being near Weaver? It isn't shown on the map."

The older man came over and glanced at the index.

"That's funny. I'm positive it's up there," he said. "I guess they most likely didn't think Belham worth showing. It's just a little place."

"But it is near Weaver?" Julia asked anxiously.

"Yep, I'd swear to that. I've never been to Belham, but I know it's pretty close to Weaver and I've been to Weaver. Not much of a town, though."

"How do I get to Weaver?" Julia asked, not letting herself seem too impatient.

"There'll be a shuttle going out of here for Weaver in about two hours," the older man said.

"Two hours? How far is Weaver from here?"

"Oh, about eighty miles."

"Do you have a bus going there?"

"Yep, but that only leaves once a day, at nine o'clock in the morning."

Julia resigned herself to spending two hours in Peabody. She was sure that once she reached Weaver, she'd find some means of transportation into Belham. She prayed that the older agent was right in his belief that Belham was near Weaver. He had to be, she told herself as she waited for the shuttle.

It was after six o'clock when she started out for Weaver. Thankfully it was summer and night fell slowly.

The shuttle was a rickety old thing that chugged along at no more than thirty or forty miles an hour. Night fell just as Julia pulled into Weaver.

The town, she saw, was no bigger than a fifty-cent piece. It was quiet, though a bit run down at the heels. Wherever she looked she saw something that needed repair. Roofs sagged, paint peeled, windows were either missing, cracked, or broken. The people themselves—few as she saw of them—seemed to be in as bad a state of repair as the town itself. Even the younger children looked old and withered. It was a depressing kind of place. She wanted to get out of it the moment she saw it. She watched a stray dog crossing the dusty street and noted that the poor animal had never learned to wag its tail.

"Excuse me," she said to a rumpled old man sitting on a straight-runged chair outside the train depot. "I'd like to make a connection for Belham. Is there a train that goes there?"

He looked up at her, eyeing her suspiciously. "Nope," he said curtly, looking away and spitting out some chewing tobacco.

Despite the answer, she felt somewhat relieved knowing that the man at least knew where Belham was. "Well, how do I get there? Is there a bus?"

"Nope." He spat again.

"Well, how *do* I get there?" she asked a little too harshly.

He turned and eyed her again. "What do you want to go there for?"

"I was born there," she said, although she'd been tempted to tell him it was none of his business.

"Oh, one of them, huh?"

"One of whom?"

He didn't answer her question. Instead he said, "Old Jerry Crow might be willing to drive you for a fee."

"And where might I find old Jerry Crow?" Julia asked, letting herself feel the satisfaction of sounding a bit sarcastic.

The sarcasm went unnoticed. "Over at the café, yonder." He pointed, which seemed to be a great effort on his part.

She thanked him curtly, picked up her luggage and started to cross the dusty road. Her muscles ached and her bags felt heavier than ever. It had been a long, long day and a long, long trip, and all her thinking had somehow managed to erase the glorious mood in which she'd awakened. She had spent too many long hours thinking about all that had happened to her. She knew she was doing the right thing because there was an invisible something telling her so, pulling her forward, luring her like a siren to the town of Belham. The black, ominous gloom which had haunted her all her life was dissolving. This had been the first day she felt totally free of everything, even herself. Despite her weariness, she could not stop, she found. She had to go on until she reached Belham.

"Where might I find Jerry Crow?" she asked a man leaning up against a sagging roof support.

"You're lookin' at 'im, Miss."

He was a tall, gangling man with dull, lifeless eyes and sunken cheeks. He looked as though he needed a good square meal as well as a shave and a hot bath. His jeans were hanging in tatters; his feet were bare.

"I was told you might drive me to Belham," Julia said.

He snapped his head around and stared at her. "I might. What do you want to go there for?"

"That's where I was born."

He gave her a suspicious look. He didn't seem to believe her, but she didn't care whether he believed her or not. "Will you drive me?" she urged.

"Ain't got no gas."

"I'll buy the gas."

"Plus forty dollars," he answered, keeping his eyes fixed firmly on hers.

"How far is it?" Forty dollars was just about every cent she had left on her.

"Oh, maybe twenty miles."

"Twenty miles? Forty dollars plus gasoline seems a bit steep to me. I'm not a millionaire, as you can see."

"Forty plus. Take it or leave it. I ain't all that keen on drivin' to Belham, especially at night."

She fumbled in her bag and handed him two twenty-dollar bills and a five. "There, that should cover everything," she said.

"The gas'll run about seven bucks," he said, fingering the five lightly.

"Well, only buy five dollars' worth. That's all the cash I have."

He kept eyeing her in that suspicious way he had. He thought for a moment and then slipped the bills into his pocket and nodded toward a sagging garage across the way. "Car's in there. I'll fetch the gas. You sit in the back and wait. I won't be long."

He was very long. Julia fidgeted and drummed her fingers on her handbag for almost half an hour before Jerry Crow arrived with a rather small can of gasoline, which Julia reminded herself had cost her five dollars.

No matter, she told herself as he poured the gas into the tank. She'd be in Belham soon and that was all that was important.

"If'n your folks are from Belham, how come they let you get away?" Jerry Crow asked while he steered the car none too carefully over a road that was no wider than a hair ribbon.

"Get away? I don't know what you mean."

He chuckled. "Oh, you know, all right." he said, eyeing her in the rearview mirror, the corner of which was chipped. "You don't have to play foxy with old Jerry Crow."

"I'm afraid I don't know what you're talking about," Julia said.

Jerry Crow chuckled again and before Julia could ask him to explain himself, he turned a sharp curve in the road and they were in Belham.

Belham was charming. The little shops and houses looked neat and strong and solid. It was dark and the lighted windows gleamed in a rosy welcome. Julia could see the straight brick chimneys jutting up against the sky, the well-tended outline of trees and shrubs. The people of Belham took obvious pride in their little town. It was no wonder the Weaverites were resentful of them. Now she understood the pointed slurs against Belham. It was plain and simple: the Weaverites were jealous, Julia decided as she mentally compared the two towns.

Jerry Crow, she noticed, looked sulkier than ever as he inched the car over the smooth, even street, brick-paved and clean-swept. "I'll take you to the inn yonder and no farther," he announced. "It ain't good for anybody to linger in Belham," he added, giving Julia a glance by way of the rearview mirror.

She merely smiled at him. She felt a wonderful sense of pride in her birthplace. "They have an inn?" she asked pleasantly.

"Yep. but they don't take no guests there. It's where they hold their meetings." He cast Julia a wary eye. A moment later he pulled the complaining old sedan up in front of a gabled building with shimmering windows and a wide door that stood fully open. He made no move to help her out or to tote her luggage, so Julia managed for herself.

She was no sooner out of the car than Jerry Crow rammed it into gear and sped away with a squeal of tires and a billow of exhaust smoke. She saw him make a wide, dangerous U-turn and race out of town with the accelerator pedal jammed to the floor.

The sound of the squealing tires and the zooming car brought several men into the doorframe. There were three of them in all, silhouetted in the light, eyes turned in the direction of Jerry Crow's fleeing automobile. As the car receded into the darkness the three pairs of eyes turned on Julia. Their stares were so frank and open they embarrassed her. She shifted her weight as she stood between her suitcases. "I'm looking for a room," she managed to say. "Mr. Crow said this was an inn."

"Aye, that it is," one of the men said, "but it don't cater to lodgers."

"At least it hasn't for a long time," another of the men said.

The third man turned his head back toward the inside light and called, "Hey, Rose. Come see what old Jerry Crow dropped on your doorstep."

A woman's shape appeared in the light. She stepped in front of the three men and stood there, hands on hips, studying Julia's face. She was a strong-looking woman, broad-hipped and gray-haired, which she wore in a tight bun at the very top of her head. The hair seemed so tightly knotted that it pulled up the corners of her eyes. The corners of her mouth, however, were pulled in the opposite direction.

"Yes?" she said sharply. "What do you want?"

Her rough manner made Julia think of the matrons back at the orphanage. She took an involuntary step backward. "I was told this was an inn," Julia stammered. "I'd like a room."

"Well, it isn't an inn. We don't take lodgers. Go away."

Julia felt panic starting to build up. Go away? Where was she to go? "But I have no place to go," Julia argued.

One of the three men peered around the heavyset woman and asked, "Where did you come from, Missy?"

The woman, Rose, spun around and gave him a withering look. "Never mind where she came from, Harold Hastings. Wherever it is, let her go back to it." She turned to Julia again. "Get away with you, girl. We want no strangers from Weaver snooping around here."

"But I'm not from Weaver. I lived in New York."

"Then go back to New York," the woman said, flinging the name at her as though it were something filthy. She planted her feet firmly beneath her and crossed her thick arms across her ample chest, ready to defend her inn against any attempt at invasion Julia might launch.

Julia stared at her, not knowing what to do. She looked toward the men, but saw there was no help in their eyes. Then she recalled a little ploy that had always worked whenever she needed to get her own way at the orphanage. It was cheating, but she had no other alternative, she decided.

"But I've come such a long, long way," she said softly, raising one hand limply to her forehead. "I've been traveling all day and without anything to eat." She let her eyes roll in her head. "Please," she said, almost in a whimper. "Please help me...."

She let her knees buckle and, as gently as she could, she let her body fall to the ground.

CHAPTER TEN

"She's coming around."

Elizabeth had said those exact words the night she fainted for real inside Madam Esperelda's tent. Julia fluttered her lids, and hoped she managed to look and sound slightly dazed.

"Where am I?" She saw the stern-looking woman, still looking stern, but less so than before.

"We carried you inside," one of the men said.

"We could hardly leave you lying out there on the street," the woman added. "You can rest here until you're strong enough to get going. I'm having some hot soup and fresh bread brought up. It'll put some strength back into you." The woman tilted her head and shook a menacing finger at Julia. "But once you're on your feet, out you go. We don't care for no strangers here."

"But if you'll just let me explain," Julia said raising her head slowly, then letting herself fall back. "I'm not a complete stranger, really. I've come to Belham to try and find my mother and father. I learned that I was born here."

She watched Rose and the men exchange looks.

"What do you mean?" the woman asked.

"My name's Julia Carson."

"There are no Carsons living in Belham. Never heard the name."

One of the old men rubbed his chin. "There was a Carson used to have the old Transberry place."

"That was Carlton," another old gent corrected.

"Oh, yeah, Carlton."

Julia said, "My mother was Bridget Bishop."

It was as if someone had stricken them all dumb. The three men and the stern-looking Rose stood there frozen in their individual attitudes. No one moved. Even their breathing seemed to stop.

"You know Bridget Bishop?" Julia asked, studying the looks of astonishment on their faces.

No one spoke for another moment and then the woman's face broke into a wide, happy grin. "Oh, my dear child," she said, going to Julia and hugging her tight.

Julia drew back in disbelief.

"So, you're Bridget's little girl? Everybody wondered what happened to you. We all thought you died when—" She cut herself off.

Julia saw her bite her tongue. Her eyes went sad. "I know my mother is dead," Julia said. "I've been in an orphanage since I was just a few days or weeks old, I understand. I was released when I became eighteen. That was two years ago."

They exchanged looks again, looks which Julia could not decipher. She saw them each nod, as though approving everything she said.

"I came to Belham on the chance that my father might still be living." She saw their faces go blank. "Wasn't my father from around here?" she asked.

No one moved for a second. Then Rose hugged her again and said, "Well, there'll be plenty of time to talk about all that later on. First, we've got to get some nourishment back into you and bring back some of the color to your cheeks. You'll meet your father soon enough, child."

"Then he does live here?"

"Yes, that he does."

Julia felt her heart jump with joy. She had a real, live father, real flesh and blood, and he was living here in Belham. Her happiness made her light-headed. "His name isn't Carson, then?" she said.

"No. That was a name the orphanage people must have

dreamed up." The girl came in with a tray and Rose took it from her and set it down on a small table near the couch on which Julia reclined. Rose busied herself spreading the napkin and arranging the various dishes on the tray. "Oh, I should have known you were Bridget's child the minute I laid eyes on you. You're the spitting image of your mother. Ah, she was a lovely thing, just like you."

Julia flushed slightly and asked, "You knew my mother well?"

"Very well," Rose said. "She was my youngest sister."

Julia had picked up a spoon but dropped it. "Then you're my aunt?" she said, beaming with joy.

"Yes, that I am. I'm your Aunt Rose. I'm afraid I'm the only family you've got, outside your father, of course. My husband, your Uncle Mack, passed away about five years ago. We never were blessed with young 'uns of our own." She jerked her head toward the three old men who stood grinning. "These old goats are the Hastings boys. They're hardly boys," she added with a short, hearty laugh, "but folks around here call them the Hastings boys, they've always called them that. This one is Harold, that's Henry, and the ugly one on the end is Herbert. It seems their pa and ma had a hankering for the letter H."

She folded her hands in front of her and laughed. "Okay, boys," she said after a moment. "You'd all better clear out and let the young lady eat in peace without your goggling at her." She shooed them away.

"Now," she said as she watched Julia spoon up the soup. "I'll go and get our front room ready for you, child." She started to leave but paused and turned back. "Who would have ever thought that this night would bring Bridget's little girl back to us. Of course, we all should have known. He told us you'd come back in time."

Julia frowned. "He? Who told you? What do you mean that I'd come back in time?" The soup was delicious and she hadn't realized how hungry she'd been. She found it difficult concentrating on both satisfying her hunger and Rose's conversation.

"Oh, enough of all that. Eat up, child. I'll tell you everything in time...or he will." She went then, skirts hiked, steps light and gay.

Julia felt light and gay, also. The soup was superb and although her little bit of trickery bothered her conscience, it had, nonetheless, served an end. Nothing, she felt, could diminish her spirits now. She'd learned that her father was still living and was here in Belham. She had a family after so long. Relatives. The word brought a wonderful throbbing to her veins. She belonged to someone. The strange ordeal had been worth every minute of the troubles she was put to, she told herself. Even the old gypsy's accusations....

"The gypsy's accusations," she said, feeling her wonderful mood slip away from her. "She'd said I was evil and trouble." She hesitated as she began to think. "My father might be an evil man. This town might well spell trouble for me." She frowned suddenly. "Or perhaps I will spell trouble for it."

Why do you persist on dwelling on the negative side of things? She asked herself. She forced herself to concentrate on her recent good fortune instead.

Aunt Rose came bustling in saying that the room was all ready for her. "And the room's right in the front where you can have a nice view of the street from your window. I had one of the Hastings boys take your bags to your room."

"Thank you, Aunt." It sounded strange calling someone "Aunt." "You're being very kind."

"And why shouldn't I be kind to my own kin, may I ask?" She put her arm around Julia's shoulder and hugged her tight. "Oh, it will be wonderful having my very own niece here with me," she said.

Julia smiled and patted her hand. She suddenly realized that she had not been the only one who'd longed for a family. Her heart went out to her Aunt Rose. They shared a common need.

Rose led her to the room. Julia tried to question her about everything, but her aunt kept putting her off, saying everything could wait until morning when Julia was rested and fresh.

Julia let herself be fussed over, complete with being tucked into bed with a loving kiss on the forehead to insure her of pleasant dreams. Despite the kiss, her dreams were far from pleasant, however.

She awoke in a tangle of bedclothes. Her body was bathed in sweat, trying to remember her nightmare, but it was gone. She lay there stiff with fear, and gradually she became aware of the sound of hoofbeats. She threw back the coverlet and padded barefoot across the floor. The smooth polished wood of the flooring felt solid and cool and reassuring.

At the window she inched back the lace curtains. There, trotting slowly down the center of the main street, was a magnificent white stallion. Sitting astride it was a tall, manly figure dressed all in black. He wore neither hood nor cape, just black riding britches and a black leather jacket. The moon glinted softly on the tips of his black, shiny boots with their silver spurs.

Julia stared, not in fear but in awe of the man. She could not see his face, but she was certain she'd know it when she saw it. It must be her father coming for her. He'd heard she arrived tonight and was coming at his first opportunity to find her and claim her.

She found herself trembling with excitement and anticipation.

The rider in black came directly up to the inn. He rode to her window and stood beneath it. He looked up and removed the cap he wore. With a gracious sweep of his arm he bowed to her, then smiled up.

A jolt of disappointment shot through Julia. The man was very young and most handsome. He was too young, however, to be her father, she saw. He was wearing a warm and affectionate smile and his eyes burned into hers as he looked up at her. As they gazed at each other, Julia got the distinct feeling that she'd seen or met the young man before, but she could not place where.

She saw his lips move. He spoke but she did not catch his words. Quickly she raised the window and leaned out. Again she saw him smile and speak, but again she did not hear any of his words. She strained her ears, but still was unable to make out what it was he was saying. It was as if she were still inside her dream. The man was addressing her, yet his words did not reach her ears. An invisible shield seemed to exist between them, a shield through which no sound was able to penetrate.

But this is no dream, she reminded herself. She was standing, shivering slightly at the open window and there was a gentleman below speaking to her. She was in Belham, Massachusetts, and it was (she turned and looked at the luminous dial of her travel alarm) three o'clock in the morning.

"Excuse me, but I cannot hear what you're saying," she called down.

The rider smiled at her again and said something. Again she did not hear him but she thought she read the word "father" on his lips.

He was bringing a message, she decided happily. He had most likely heard about her arriving at the inn and was carrying a message from her father.

"Wait, I'll be right down," she called as she hurried into slippers and a quilted robe. She gave no heed to the possibility of danger. It was all as she believed it to be. The young man was a messenger sent from her father. Her father couldn't come himself but wanted her to know that he'd been informed of her arrival. She was convinced that that was what it was all about.

She opened her door softly and trotted down the wooden stairs to the main level of the inn. She went directly to the front door and, finding it unlocked and unbolted, went outside. She looked up and down the main street. She walked beneath her own bedroom window.

There was no one there. The street was completely deserted.

CHAPTER ELEVEN

It took her a long time to fall asleep, but when she did she slept soundly, undisturbed by further nightmares or men on galloping stallions.

In the morning she lay thinking of the strange man who had disappeared practically before her eyes. She had not heard him gallop away. He had vanished into thin air, it seemed. She held fast to the belief that he had been sent by her father. She was positive she'd seen the word "father" formed by his lips during his silent speech. She'd find her father, wherever he was, and the riddle of the rider in black would most likely have a very simple explanation.

Aunt Rose tapped at the door and opened it without waiting for an invitation. "Well, I see you're wide awake," she said. "Did you sleep well, child?"

Julia stretched. "After a fashion," she said. "I had the most awful nightmare, though."

"Girls as young and pretty as you aren't supposed to have nightmares," Aunt Rose said, turning to straighten the things on the bureau.

"Not only did I have a nightmare, but I also had a visit from a very handsome young man on a white horse."

Her aunt stopped fussing with the things on the bureau and turned sharply. "What is that you say?"

Julia was smiling. "I said I had a middle-of-the-night visit from a rather handsome young gentleman on a white charger."

Aunt Rose's eyes widened. She stared at Julia with what Julia interpreted as puritan disapproval. Julia laughed. "Oh, Aunt, it was nothing like that. I awoke to the sound of a horse's hooves on the street outside. I went to investigate and I saw a man dressed in black, seated astride a white horse standing below my window. He spoke to me but, oddly enough, I could not hear what he said. It was as if he spoke into a vacuum. So I put on a robe and slippers and went downstairs and outside. By the time I got outside to where he'd been standing, he was gone, vanished. What is it, Aunt? You look quite strange. Are you feeling all right?"

Aunt Rose pulled herself together. Again she resumed fussing with the things on the bureau. "It's nothing," she said hastily. But Julia sensed by her sudden nervous actions that something she'd said had upset her aunt. "Do you know this man whom my father sent to me last night?"

"I don't know," Aunt Rose said, not turning. "You'd better get yourself up and dressed. You'll be wanting to go to your father's place. I suppose he knows you've arrived. News here in Belham travels like wildfire."

"If my father knows I'm here, why hasn't he shown up to meet me?" Julia knit her brows. "Perhaps he doesn't want me. I never thought that he may not want a daughter."

"Of course your father wants you. The man was half-crazed when you and your mother disappeared. Then when Bridget's body was brought back and they said they took you away from her, I thought the man would kill the lot of them."

"They? Who took me away from my mother?"

Aunt Rose brushed an imaginary piece of lint from her dark skirt. "The people in charge of Bridget, of course."

"In charge of her? I don't understand."

Aunt Rose heaved a sigh. "Well, I suppose it's up to me to tell you, being as I'm your mother's only sister. You'll have to know sooner or later. You're a grown woman now, so I don't see any harm in your knowing."

"Knowing what?"

Aunt Rose grinned slyly. "Your sweet and innocent mother

died in jail. Oh, everybody said it wasn't poor Bridget's fault, the trouble she got herself into. And before anybody could get help, Bridget up and died and they took her baby—you—and we never knew where they took you to. They wouldn't tell us."

"Who are *they*?" Julia asked.

Her aunt gave an impatient wave of her arm. "But you mustn't be thinking about Bridget. Your mother wasn't the best of women, but she could have ended up better. Those people over in Weaver were out looking for a kind of revenge. They got revenge, all right," she said, her eyes shiny and glassy. "We're a simple folk here and we never did a lick of harm to anyone from Weaver. Nonetheless, they laid hands on Bridget one night out on the road. She was carrying you. They took her and made wild accusations. Then they...Bridget died and we thought they killed you, too."

Julia gasped. "Killed? They killed my mother?"

Aunt Rose shrugged indifferently. "Oh, I guess I shouldn't have let that slip out. None of us are positive they actually killed poor Bridget, but there's a lot of us think they did, if you must know the truth. Of course, the people in Weaver claimed she just up and died, but we never believed them, any of us."

Julia was horror-struck. "This is monstrous," she gasped

Aunt Rose merely shrugged and looked undisturbed. "It was a long time ago, girl. It all happened so quickly that it was over before we knew what had happened. One day Bridget was gone, and the next, she was dead and her child had vanished."

"But surely the police investigated?"

"There isn't much law and order here. Oh, we have a sheriff of sorts. So does Weaver, but they're just part-time jobs. There's no money to pay for real law and order. Nearest law establishment is in Peabody."

"Well, why didn't you go to Peabody and have them come and look into the matter?"

"That wasn't necessary. We took care of it all by ourselves. You're a stranger in these parts, girl. You'll learn after a while that we look after our own. Outsiders are no more welcome in

Belham than they are in Weaver. It's been like that since the towns' beginnings and that's the way we want it. We take care of our own justice in our own way."

"But you just allowed Bridget's child to vanish without looking for it."

"He looked for you. He was told not to, but he searched for a while and then gave up."

"What do you mean, he was told not to."

"Just that."

"I don't understand any of this," Julia said, feeling quite frustrated.

"There's not much to understand. We got satisfaction for your mother's death."

"Revenge? Surely you don't believe that revenge is the answer?"

"It's the only answer in these parts. That's the way of things around here and there's no changing them. An eye for an eye and all that. That's what we believe."

"But that's barbaric."

"Well, child, now you know it all. I hadn't intended telling you all this, but it just popped out before I could catch it. No matter. I suppose sooner is better than later."

"I must find my father," Julia said.

"Of course you must. His house is hard to miss. It's the big gabled one at the very end of town. It sits practically in the middle of the road. Your father was never one for trying to hide himself. A fine, wonderful man, your father. Tall and bold and brave. Yes, indeed, a wonderful man. You must go to him. He'd never come here to you, even knowing you were here."

"Why? Why wouldn't he come here to me?"

"He just wouldn't. He is a proud gent. He seldom ventures into this part of town. He lives with his housekeeper and never bothers anybody. He's generous to a fault, though, and there isn't a man, woman, or child in Belham who wouldn't gladly cut out their hearts for him. Yes, indeed, a good man, your father. You're a lucky child, you are."

CHAPTER TWELVE

The house was as Aunt Rose had said: impossible to miss.

It was a huge, dark affair with multiple turrets and porches, gables and archways. Its clapboard sides were painted a dark shade of gray, its shutters black. A gate, dominating the iron-spear fence, stood open, and as Julia walked through it, she experienced a strange sensation. It was as though she had stepped from one world into another. The air itself seemed different.

There was no bell. The door knocker was in the shape of a ram's head, with tiny eyes made of some dark material set into the bronze metal; the eyes seemed to be watching her. A large bronze ring hung suspended from the ram's nostrils. Julia lifted the ring and let it bang down. The whole house seemed to vibrate from the sound. Julia held her breath. This was the end of her long, long search. Finally it was finished. She was home. She was where she belonged, where she was needed and wanted.

The door remained closed and Julia's pulse throbbed more quickly. Again she raised the knocker and let it bang down. This time she did it with more determination. And again the deep, thick thud of the ring hitting against its solid plate send a thundering boom throughout the rambling old mansion.

Finally the door opened on silent, well-oiled hinges. Julia found herself facing a rather tall, somewhat austere-looking woman with gray hair that flew in every direction. Her eyes were narrowed into a squint, the chin was pointed and her nose was sharp-ridged and crooked. "Well?" the old woman croaked.

Julia tried a weak little smile. "I'm looking for...." She fell silent. Who was she looking for? No one had thought to tell her her father's name. It wasn't Carson, like her own; that much she'd been told.

Was it Bishop? She felt most foolish, standing there with open mouth and motionless tongue. She couldn't just tell this strange old woman that she was looking for her father.

"I'm sorry," Julia stammered. "I seem to be in a quandary."

The old woman put her bony hands on her hips and tilted her head to an impatient angle. "Who is it you want, girl?"

"I'm Bridget Bishop's daughter," Julia managed to say.

She saw the old woman's expression change. The weary old eyes brightened for a moment, then narrowed again as she looked Julia up and down. She stared into her face for a full minute then said, "Yes, I heard you'd come to Belham. You got her eyes and her hair. She was prettier, though...had more meat on her." She moved aside with a quick shuffling little step. "Well, come in, girl, come in. Don't stand out there for all the people to gawk at. He isn't home, went out early this morning... never said where he was going...never does," the old woman ushered Julia into the house and carefully, solidly closed and locked the door.

Julia found herself standing in the center of a massive labyrinth of rooms, corridors, and staircases. It was as if she stood in the hub of a giant wheel with passageways going off in every direction. The inside was as gray and bleak as the outside. The foyer into which she'd been admitted was a large circle with a stairway that curved up one wall and down the other. The old woman must have noticed Julia's interest in the horseshoe staircase.

"The living go up the right; the dead come down the left," she muttered with a cackle.

One lone reception table stood in the very center of the foyer. On it was a single urn filled to overflowing with dried stalks and flowers in autumnal colors. The chandelier overhead was of polished brass which had been curled and spiralled and twisted into the most intricate of designs. The floor was black, the walls were stretched with silver-gray silk. The carpeting on the stairs was blood red. Julia found the whole atmosphere depressing.

"Have you had your breakfast, Miss?" the old woman asked.

"Thank you, yes. What time will my father be back, do you think?"

The woman lifted one bony shoulder higher than the other. "With him there's no way of knowing. In all the years I've served him, he still tells me nothing. He'll be here when he gets here, that's all I can tell you." She nodded toward double doors. "You can wait in there. It's the parlor. That's the only room we keep up these days. The rest of the place is going to wrack and ruin. It'll all fall down around our ears if we're not careful."

The room Julia entered was pleasant enough. At least the colors were a bit brighter, but not much more. These walls were stretched with powder-blue linen. The rugs were deep, deep purple, the draperies heavy black. There were white accents here and there, but overall, the room seemed one large portion of purple and black, suspended in light blue.

"Well, make yourself as cozy as you can, Miss. Ring if you need anything," the old woman said, nodding toward a bell-pull next to an ornate black-marble fireplace. "They call me Matilda."

"Thank you, Matilda. Truthfully, I don't know what my real name is now. I've been called Julia Carson, but I suppose my real name is Bishop...like his," she added, hoping the old woman would enlighten her.

"He never misses lunch, so at least you know you'll not have to wait all day." She cackled again and shuffled out of the room, leaving Julia very much alone.

She went toward the window, figuring to open the draperies and admit some daylight. She found, however, that the seams had been solidly stitched together. How curious, she thought as she felt for the dividing seams. She found none.

Tucked in one dark corner of the room was a statue of an unusual size and shape. The dimness of the corner made it unrecognizable. Julia walked toward it, and as she got closer she continued to have difficulty identifying the piece of sculpture. It was neither male nor female in gender, nor was it animal or human, but a combination thereof. The figure stood almost six-feet high, she calculated, with a head much too out of proportion to the rest of the body. The statue was carved from dark stone, marble perhaps, she decided. And down the front of the torso was a gold overlay, applied in layers to resemble feathers, fur, or fish scales. The face was hideous. Bright yellow eyes peered out from the black face, if one could call it a face. Where the nose should have been was a long snout like that of a very large dog; where the hair should have been was a mane with stubby horns at the forelocks. The figure had arms and hands, but glancing down at the feet, Julia saw that it stood on paws with long, sharp claws.

She touched the golden staff it held in one hand. To her amazement, the arm moved slightly and she heard a scraping sound as a portion of the wall behind the strange statue slid open. A large cavernous room appeared to the rear.

If the statue bewildered her, the room proved even more perplexing. The center of the room was completely empty, a vast oval space with black-marble flooring. At one end of the oval was a raised platform on which stood what looked like an altar of sorts. Candlesticks were placed in a row atop the flat slab.

She remembered Miss Marshall's cigarette lighter was still in her handbag. She rummaged in the bag for it and, finding it, flicked it on and lit one of the tall candles. The flame flickered and grew tall and straight in the almost airless room, sending long, ominous shadows stretching into the blackness.

Julia glanced around the room. The place was draped completely in black, which accounted for the lack of draft and the dense silence that hung over everything. Around the outside of the oval were statues of strange forms, none of which were identifiable. There were animals or mixtures of men and beasts, huge birds, reptiles that stood on their tails, naked monsters that made the blood rush to her temples and force her to look away from their grotesque attitudes.

Behind the statues, the draperies were hung with hideous pictures of burning cities, faces with hair on fire, crosses turned upside down. She turned back toward the altar and raised her tall candlestick. Over the altar was a massive face with bright, gleaming yellow eyes, pointed ears and sharp stabbing horns on the forehead. Julia felt cold fear catch in her throat. She dropped the candle, throwing the room back into darkness. Turning, she blindly dashed out.

Her breath was short and she leaned, unknowingly, against the old statue that stood guarding the entrance to the room. Unwittingly she touched the arm and heard the wall paneling slide shut.

Why would anyone want so hideous a room? What kind of a man was her father? The inverted crucifixes, the burning cities, all made her think of the powers of hell that the medium had referred to. Was she never to escape this evil that seemed to be pursuing her?

She couldn't stay here. No, she decided. She'd go now and perhaps return another time when she had a chance to gather her wits and nerves about her.

Just as she started for the door again, a figure, tall and straight and masculine, loomed before her.

"So you are the daughter I have been searching and waiting for all these years," the man said.

His voice was the softest, smoothest, most charming, and beautiful voice Julia had ever heard.

CHAPTER THIRTEEN

Her heart in her throat, Julia stared up at the lean, handsome face with eyes so soft and sparkling they took her breath away. His lips, full and delicate, were curved in a most inviting smile. He was clean-shaven, with dark hair silvered at the temples. He towered over her. Looking up, Julia never remembered ever seeing a mature man as handsome as this. She found she could not speak.

"They call you Julia, I understand," he said in his deep, lush, resonant tone. He raised his arms and opened them wide. "Haven't you a kiss for the father who lived only for this day?"

Julia felt the stinging behind her eyes. She swayed forward and found herself collapsing in her father's strong, comforting embrace. The house, the room, the atmosphere were all swept magically into oblivion as she gave herself up to her tears of happiness. She pressed hard against him, welcoming his protective strength. He smoothed her hair and pressed his lips to her temples and hugged her tight.

"My daughter, my daughter," he breathed.

"Oh, Father," she sobbed, and then her voice faltered again.

"You have no idea how long I have waited for this moment," her father said. "I searched and searched but without success, as well you know. Oh, my dearest little girl, how wonderful for you to have found me. I had all but given you up."

"I always knew I'd find you someday," she said. "It was as if some invisible force was leading me to you ever since they discharged me from the orphanage."

"Orphanage? Ah, I see. No wonder we could find no trace of you. All we learned was that they spirited you away. Everyone said you had died with your mother, but I refused to believe that." Again he hugged her. "But all that is in the past now. We must try to forget our loneliness. We have each other at last. Nothing will take you away from me again. Come, let us have Matilda prepare us some lunch. We have a lot to say to one another." He pulled the bell cord and when the old woman appeared, he told her to fix lunch for two. When they were again alone, he kissed Julia's forehead and led her to a large divan that faced a dead fireplace. He reached for her hand as they settled themselves.

"Now," he started, "I want to know all about you...where you've been, how you've lived...and especially how you came to find me after all these years. You know, Julia, you are very much like your mother. Perhaps even more beautiful. I am very proud indeed to be your father."

"And I your daughter," Julia said softly. She gave a little laugh. "You would not believe the things I was thinking earlier. I was certain you would not want to see a daughter you scarcely knew. I was sure you'd reject me and order me out of your house."

"My dear child," he said, patting her hand. "I would never reject you. I have lived for this day. I spent a long time searching for you, but as the years passed the trail grew too cold to follow. I knew, though, that we would find each other someday." He paused and looked deep into Julia's face. "Tell me how you did come to find me when my search for you proved so fruitless."

"Oh, it's a long story. But I suppose it was destiny or fate that brought me here. Strange, now that I think of it, I suppose I too always knew we'd find each other. I never really believed them when they told me I had neither father nor mother. They said that my parents were dead, but I never accepted that. I had the strangest feeling that someone was always behind me, leading me to you. Then, when I was discharged from the orphanage at eighteen, I went to New York. I suppose it was fate again that led me there because I made friends with three girls from my office. I really shouldn't say I made friends with them, though, because we were never all that friendly toward each other. But oddly enough, I found myself on vacation with them one week. It was as if some strange, magnetic force was pulling me closer and closer to you. It was one of the girls who suggested the crystal-ball gazer."

"The crystal-ball gazer?" Her father laughed.

Julia flushed slightly and grinned. "Yes. Believe it or not, a fortune teller was the one who started me on the path to finding you here in Belham."

"A fortune teller. How wonderful."

"She really wasn't all that wonderful. She said some awful things about me and I had a terrible experience with her, but in the end she proved responsible for my being here."

"Well, pay no attention to whatever she said to upset you. We owe her a vote of thanks."

"Strange," she said, "but I just had the oddest feeling that we've met before somewhere."

"It was your subconscious dictating to you. Away back in your infancy you most likely harbored a vision of me of which you were not conscious. The mind is a very complicated and intriguing piece of machinery that begins operating the moment we take our first breath of life—and some say even before that. The mind is capable of much more than we can imagine." Smoothing back her hair, he kissed her forehead again. "Try not to think of anything that might disturb you, my pet. Forget the past. We have a whole new future waiting before us."

Julia smiled.

"What name do you go by?" her father asked.

"Julia Carson."

"Hmmmm. The name we gave you was that of your mother, Bridget Bishop." He grinned. "I suppose it would be rather nonsensical to call you Bridget when you've grown so accustomed to Julia."

"No. I really wouldn't mind at all," she said. "Bridget is such a beautiful name."

"Nevertheless," he said, "I insist you keep Julia." He paused and added, "But the Carson must go. You must have your own true name."

"Julia Bishop?" Julia said.

Her father chuckled again. "I hate to confuse you totally, but actually your name is not Bishop either. That was the name which I was known by when your mother and I married. Since then I have reverted back to using my original family name. Cagliostro. I, your father, am the direct descendant of the infamous Count Cagliostro. "

"Cagliostro?"

"Dr. Lucius Cagliostro, at your service," he said with a flourish. "And you are my only daughter, Julia Cagliostro. You've heard of Count Cagliostro, I presume?"

Julia shook her head. "No," she said simply.

He laughed again. "Then you must read all about him. He was quite a scoundrel." His eyes twinkled merrily. "He was my great-great-grandfather...or was he my great-great-great-grandfather? Anyway, you'll find him a fascinating old tyrant, and most disreputable."

He leaned back against the couch cushions and regarded Julia for a moment. "You see, when my parents brought me to this country, the name Cagliostro had a very bad reputation. My father decided to change our name from Cagliostro to something else. On the boat over, the first man he spoke to was a Bishop, so my father—being a rather simple man—chose the name Bishop as our family name. They were afraid of the evil gossip which always seemed to follow the name Cagliostro around. My ancestors were always subjected to troublesome gossip whenever people spoke of them."

"Evil gossip?" Julia felt a sudden chill. Daughter of evil, she thought.

"Oh, it is really nothing. All legend and fantasy and silly superstition. It was just that the old count did not enjoy the best reputation among his vassals, and they concocted a lot of terrible tales that were handed down from generation to generation. But being a modem-thinking individual, when I found myself without wife or child, I decided I would adopt my true family name. People around here have accepted the change, and I am happy being who I was intended to be."

Julia found herself nodding. "Yes, I can readily understand the desire to own your rightful name, regardless of what it may be," she said.

"But in your case, you were christened Bridget Bishop. If you wish to retain title name Bishop, it is all right with me, although I would, of course, prefer you adopt your father's true name, Cagliostro. It would please me very much."

"Julia Cagliostro," she said with a grin. "I'll have to learn to spell it, but it does have a lovely sound to it."

"Good, then it is settled. The lovely Julia is reinstated with her father, and the Cagliostro name will be carried on to future generations." He gave her a sidelong look. "I was afraid the name might end with me."

Julia's face went red. "I hadn't given any thought to marrying. The prospects in Belham must be rather slim." She suddenly remembered the handsome young rider on the white horse who had appeared beneath her window during the night.

"You need not worry about finding a husband," he told her. "One as beautiful as you will have no trouble. If you find no one to suit you here in Belham, we are free to travel. Of course, we must always keep this as our home."

Julia frowned, remembering the strange secret room she had discovered earlier.

"What is it, child? Is it that you do not wish to make this your home?"

Julia shook her head. "No, it isn't that." She hesitated. "I like Belham well enough, it's just...." Unconsciously her eyes wandered around the room and came to rest on the weird statue tucked away in the corner.

Her father saw where she looked and laughed. "If anything in the house displeases you, we will have it changed. I have lived alone for too many years with my collection and only Matilda to worry about. I suppose this room, this house, is a bit grim in the eyes of a young, lovely girl such as you. Do what you wish to change it to suit you, but I must ask that you do respect some of my priceless possessions, such as that piece of sculpture which made you frown."

Her father rose and crossed to the hideous thing that stood in its corner. "I collect old and unusual idols, such as this," he said. "This is a very important Egyptian god. His name is Anubis," he announced with obvious pride. "Anubis, the jackal god, aids the pharaohs who died in the underworld. He holds a divine scepter and guards the sacred underworld from all unworthy intruders."

Julia felt a tinge of guilt knowing that she ranked as an intruder, if indeed the room beyond was her father's so-called underworld. "Then you are an archaeologist?" she said, trying to hide her guilt.

"Oh, no. Ancient cultures are a hobby of mine, no more. I'm interested in all the people of the world." He came back and sat down beside her again. "This house is crammed full with my collection of idols, icons, tapestries, paintings, sculptures from almost every culture that ever existed."

Julia thought again of the secret room and was going to speak of it but glanced at the statue of Anubis and remembered her father's words: "...guards...from all unworthy intruders." She decided to say nothing of her having found the hidden room.

So it was all a hobby, as she had suspected. She felt much better about living here. She would brighten up the place with Matilda's help. It wouldn't be all that bad after she'd had a chance to bring in some freshness.

"I promise not to depose any of your gods or goddesses," she told her father. "And I know I'll be very happy living here with you." She snuggled close to him. "I've never had a real home before. Now that I have, I don't want to leave it."

"We are together now and there is nothing on this earth that can separate us. The Cagliostros were always a noble, proud, and determined family. We will not dishonor the name by being otherwise. If it is your wish to remain here in Belham, then so be it; however, we must travel and broaden your education and knowledge of things. The world is a wide and wonderful and strange place. I want you to know it well." He turned his head and studied her for a moment. "Your age, child? I believe you must be near twenty-one. I'm afraid I lost count. It has been a long time."

"I'll be twenty-one on the first of September according to the records at the orphanage."

"Ah, but that is not correct. You were born in August. It was very hot, I remember. Your poor mother was so uncomfortable. I asked for a cool breeze to comfort her and the powers that be heard my plea." He knit his brows. "The thirteenth of August. Yes, I'm positive it was the thirteenth of August. Your birth certificate is somewhere in my papers. I'll search it out and confirm my memory. The orphanage most likely got you on the first of September and adopted that as your birthday. Your mother and you disappeared very shortly after you were born... only a few weeks. You were such a tiny little thing...and so very pretty."

"I never did feel much like a Virgo," Julia said with a smile.

"No, child. You are a Leo child—strong and powerful and determined."

"My mother," Julia said after a pause. "Aunt Rose told me she died in the Weaver jail."

"Your Aunt Rose is a fool," her father snapped, growing suddenly irritable. "Your mother died in Weaver, true enough, but not in their jail."

Julia frowned. "I don't understand. Why would she tell me such a terrible thing if it were not true?"

Her father gave her a kindly look. "The truth is, Julia, that your mother was running away from me. She died near Weaver. Somehow you were taken away from her, and no one knew who took you or where you were taken. After you were born, your mother grew very ill. She suffered fits of delirium. She did not know she was running from me, or that she was carrying you with her."

He shook his head. "It was a very sad day for me when they returned her body here to Belham and we found you were gone. Very sad indeed," he said. Then he brightened. "But let us not talk of your mother and such sad things now. You are here. All that is in the past. Everything is fine again. You have been returned to me, and from now on we will only laugh and think of wonderful, pleasant things." He paused again, as though disturbed by a sudden thought. "You are staying at the inn?"

"Yes. Aunt Rose took me in last night, although I had to pretend to faint before she did so. She's made me most comfortable."

"But you will not stay there. I will have your things brought here. This is your home. I will have you living nowhere else. We can send for whatever you left behind in New York. This is your home from now on."

"I'd like that," Julia found herself saying, despite all the misgivings she had had about the gloomy old house and the strange, black secret room. All she wanted was to be with her father. That was all she cared about now.

"That is settled then. Come, we will have our lunch and get you settled in immediately thereafter. Your aunt is a wonderful, kind woman, but she is prone to be a bit of a gossip and a troublemaker. I would prefer you do not place much importance on anything she says. She tends to be overly dramatic at times."

They got up from the couch and started toward where Julia imagined the dining room was located. "Incidentally," she said as they crossed the large, dismal foyer with its horseshoe staircase, "I had a visit from a man on horseback during the night. I believe he was sent by you. Was he?"

Her father put back his head and laughed. "If it was who I think it was, he lost no time in reaching you. In the middle of the night, you say?"

"Yes, it was about three in the morning. I woke up and heard the sound of hoofbeats on the street outside. And there he was under my window, sitting astride a white horse."

"How like him," he said. "How very much like him, the young devil." He laughed again and slid open the big double doors leading to the dining room. "Shall we eat, child? I'm famished."

CHAPTER FOURTEEN

During lunch her father talked of his travels throughout the world. It seemed there wasn't a corner of it that he did not know. Julia sat, fascinated by his wonderful stories.

"I have work to do in my study, Julia," he told her as they lingered over the fresh fruit sherbet. "I'll have someone bring your things from the inn." He suddenly looked stern for a moment. "Incidentally, pay no attention to what your aunt says. She tends to speak harshly about your mother, which I do not particularly appreciate, but under the circumstances...." He fanned out his hands in a helpless gesture.

"Aunt Rose didn't like my mother, did she?"

"Your aunt lives in a strange world all her own. She persists in concocting insane stories without thinking. I'm sure she has already told you some wild tale about Bridget."

"She told me that she was killed, murdered by the people in Weaver."

He shook his head again. "Yes, I thought as much. It isn't the first time I've heard that. And if you are around her often enough, she will get around to telling you that your mother was burned at the stake. She's told that to others."

"But why does she say such dreadful things?"

"The poor woman is to be pitied. She is not altogether sound. She was always envious of your beautiful mother, and I believe she is still envious of her, even after death." He pushed back his chair and got quickly to his feet. "But enough talk about such morbidity on such a wonderful day. I must go and find someone to fetch your luggage."

Without thinking Julia said, "The man who visited me last night...."

Her father laughed. "No, I'm afraid that handsome young devil isn't available. He's a strange one, he is. I never know when or where he'll show up."

"Who is he?"

"Oh, you'll meet him in due time."

"Does he work for you?"

"In a manner of speaking, yes. But only part-time. And don't ask me his name or anything about him, because I couldn't tell you. He comes and he goes. He's most unusual. I never know where he goes or when he comes. One day he'll be here and the next he'll be gone."

"I assume you sent him to my window last night?"

"We spoke of you, but he had no direct order from me. His calling on you was his own idea, obviously. I think he was anxious to get a look at you. He's rather a romantic fellow." He laughed.

Julia blushed.

"You don't mind going to the inn alone, do you, Daughter? I never venture into town unless it is an absolute emergency."

"No, of course not. I can find my way quite easily."

"Good. Get your things together and leave them in your room. I'll have one of the men fetch them here. Now, get along with you. I want you settled here as soon as possible."

Julia went directly back to the inn. She didn't want to see her Aunt Rose, but she knew it would be impossible to avoid her.

"Well, I assume you found each other without any trouble," her aunt said when Julia entered the inn.

"Yes," Julia answered, sounding pleasant. "Thank you."

"A wonderful man, your father. Didn't you find him wonderful?"

"Yes. wonderful."

"He'll want you to move in, I suppose."

"That is what I intend doing now. He wanted me to pack and

he'll send someone for my bags."

"Good, good; that's as it should be." Her Aunt Rose gave a little chuckle. "Weird old house, isn't it? I hope it didn't frighten you. It's very strange and takes getting used to."

"Yes," Julia said, not wanting to invite conversation. She started up the stairs. She knew she was being purposely curt, but she found she could not help thinking about the terrible things her aunt had said about her mother. Knowing Rose's dislike of her mother, Julia wanted to be away from her.

"What's wrong?" Aunt Rose asked, stopping Julia midway up the stairs.

"Nothing. What could be wrong?"

"You're acting rather strangely toward me. What did he tell you?"

"Tell me? I don't understand."

"He said something bad about me, didn't he?"

"No," Julia said.

"You're lying."

Julia felt flustered. She turned and went up the stairs to her room. Aunt Rose dashed after her.

"Did your father stick up for that mother of yours?" Aunt Rose demanded.

"Please, Aunt Rose. I don't wish to discuss my mother."

"So he did!"

Aunt Rose suddenly burst into tears. "He told me he loved me," she whimpered. She gave Julia a helpless look, then turned and slowly walked from the room with shoulders drooping and head bowed.

Julia finished packing and snapped shut her bag. She was ready to start her new life. She was going home.

When she came down, Aunt Rose was sitting in a chair near the front door. "You'll come and see me now and then, Julia?"

Julia nodded and smiled, but she knew she would not.

"I know he never really loved me as I love him," her aunt said. "Try not to think too harshly of a foolish old woman like me." She went to Julia and kissed her on the cheek. "I forgot myself for a moment. I am very glad you're here. We've been waiting for you for a long time."

* * * * * * *

Matilda handed her a door key when she arrived home.

"We thought you should have this, but your father said you must not wander out alone too often."

Julia took the key and dropped it into her handbag without giving it a second thought. "Where is my father now?"

"In his study. I wouldn't suggest you disturb him, though. He likes to enjoy his privacy in there. He'll come out when he's ready. In the meantime, I'd suggest you leave him be. He gave me strict orders never to interrupt him under any circumstances when his study doors are closed."

"I'll remember that," Julia said.

"Come. Let me show you the room I've been getting ready for you. I'm afraid it's in a real mess, because I haven't had much time, you only arriving this morning and all."

"Now, don't start fussing over me, Matilda. I can get my room ready."

They started up the one side of the horseshoe staircase.

"Speaking of rooms," Julia said, "I really would like to put some color into this place. Everything is so dark and drab and dreary."

Matilda cackled. "He said you'd be changing a few things around. Don't get too ambitious, though. The doctor isn't all that keen on change."

"The doctor?"

"Your father, Dr. Cagliostro."

"Oh, of course. How foolish of me. He did tell me his full name. Lucius, isn't it?" Before Matilda could confirm, Julia added, "Is he a medical doctor?"

"Oh, no. He's one of those scientific ones. Well, here's where he wants you," Matilda said as she pushed open a heavy oak door. "His rooms are just across the hall."

"Why, it's charming...or will be," Julia said.

"Yes, once we get it cleaned up and fixed up nice," the old woman said as she started pulling dust covers from chairs.

It was indeed a lovely room, but a strange one, Julia noted. The skeleton of a huge bed dominated one wall. Its trappings had all been removed, leaving only the posts that ran upward supporting the frame for a canopy. The windows were draped in a golden material that was faded and old and heavy with dust. The floor was of colored marble scattered with Persian rugs, all very worn and dirty-looking. The walls were patterned with a print paper but here and there, niches were cut, niches which once held statues or lamps, but which were all empty now. Cartons of books, papers, and an assortment of other debris cluttered up the place..

"Oh, it will be very handsome once it's fixed up," Julia said as she inspected the view from the mullion windows. "I'll do it in bright yellows and oranges. And these rugs must definitely go. And white, I think for the bed. Don't you agree, Matilda?"

"Whatever you say, Miss Julia. It's where he wants you, and he says whatever you want you must have."

Julia wrapped her arms around herself and spun around. "Am I prejudiced, Matilda, or is my father truly a wonderful man?"

"You're not prejudiced, Miss Julia. No finer man exists. The doctor is a prince. We wouldn't all be here if it wasn't for him."

Julia glanced at her. "What do you mean?"

Matilda was folding the dust covers. "It's just that the whole town of Belham would fall apart if anything ever happened to Doctor Cagliostro."

"I don't understand. Why do they all depend on him?"

"Because he's Doctor Cagliostro." The old woman shrugged. "That's reason enough."

"I must read about the Cagliostros now that I am one of them," Julia said. "Are there any books about his...I mean, my family anywhere in the house?"

"Oh, my, yes. The library downstairs has several volumes on your ancestors. Some of them are written in funny languages which I couldn't make hide nor hair of. But they're in the library for anybody to read who's interested."

Julia made a mental note of searching them out. She was very interested.

Her breast was bursting with happiness as she and Matilda spent the rest of the afternoon straightening and cleaning and planning on what colors the walls were to be and where to find the shag carpeting Julia decided she wanted for the floor.

By five she was completely done in. Matilda went to see about preparing dinner and Julia soaked herself for half an hour in a steaming tub of water. Then she changed into a light print dress and went to find Matilda in the kitchen. She had no trouble finding her way back downstairs but once there, she stood looking around, trying to decide in which direction she might find Matilda.

As she stood in the foyer, she noticed that the doors to the parlor were open. Seeing them reminded her that she'd left evidence of her presence in the secret room. The discarded candlestick was still lying in the middle of the floor where she'd dropped it.

Quietly she went through the parlor and touched the arm of the statue of Anubis. The panel slid open and Julia hurried through. She did not give much thought to the weird statues or the frightening paintings and tapestries now. She found the candle, replaced it on the altar slab and turned to leave.

Hurrying back toward the light of the parlor, she stopped suddenly and thought she heard movement coming from behind her. She looked around. There was no one to be seen. She quickened her steps. How deadly silent the room was, she thought. The heavy black draperies even silenced her footsteps on the black-marble flooring. Again she heard a sound. She stood still; she was positive there was someone behind her. She knew her instincts well and they never lied to her.

She turned back again and looked toward the altar. She saw the shape of a man move into the shadows. She strained to make him out. He'd moved quickly, but not quickly enough. She wasn't mistaken. It had been the outline of the man in black who'd appeared beneath her window at the inn.

She didn't feel there was anything to fear now that her father had explained everything. She could easily explain how she had stumbled onto the secret room quite by accident. She decided she wanted to meet the young man, but just then she heard a door open and close somewhere outside the room. It made her pause and consider. Her father might be angry with her for having trespassed into one of his possible sanctuaries. She didn't want to do anything to make him annoyed with her. Quickly she skirted the statue of Anubis, touched the arm, and the panel slid shut.

A moment later, Dr. Lucius Cagliostro entered the parlor.

"There you are, child," he said. He came toward her and embraced her. "And how have you spent your afternoon?"

She glanced at the closed panel and thought of the man she'd seen there. "Matilda and I have been making up my room," she told him. "I'm afraid I have rather ambitious plans for it."

"Good. Spare no expense. Whatever you wish will be yours. Nothing is too good for the daughter of Dr. Lucius Cagliostro."

CHAPTER FIFTEEN

He was distressed to hear of all her unhappy years at the orphanage. But Julia did not dwell very long on those unhappy times. She wanted to forget the orphanage, the miseries she had suffered at the hands of Miss Marshall and the other matrons. She coaxed her father to tell her of his work, his travels, and he in turn asked her about her studies and ambitions.

"I have had only one major ambition in my lifetime," she told him. "That was to find you."

He gave her a kindly smile. "Then you must set a new ambition for yourself, Daughter. You have found me and we will never be separated again."

"What ambition would you suggest I set?" she asked.

"To marry, of course. I must have grandchildren. You must continue the Cagliostro name."

"But they will have my husband's name when they are born."

Her father waved his hand as though she had placed a rather unimportant obstacle in his path. "That is merely a technicality which can be easily remedied. As long as the children have my blood, they will be Cagliostros."

It was the first time Julia had ever afforded herself the luxury of speaking of marriage and children. She remembered all the parentless waifs who were filtered through the orphanage, and made a silent vow that her children would never be one of their number. Perhaps one day it might be possible to adopt little Meg. But glancing at her father, she doubted if he would take too kindly to having other family blood mixed with their own.

The evening passed too quickly. The large clock in the foyer struck ten and her father pushed himself up out of his easy chair. "I, for one, have had a very busy and delightful day. I'm off to bed. You should think about retiring also, Julia. You must be completely exhausted."

Julia hugged herself. "I'm too happy and contented to sleep. Perhaps I'll read about our family for a while before turning in."

He kissed the top of her head. "The library is just across the hall. But don't strain your lovely eyes on Cagliostro history. There is plenty of time for you to learn about your ancestors."

He left her and she sat for a long time dreaming of how fortunate she was. She even smiled at thoughts of Madam Esperelda and her overly dramatic demonstration. A worried little frown suddenly tugged at her brow as she remembered the medium's pointing finger.

"Daughter of evil."

Julia shook herself and got up from her chair. She crossed the foyer, refusing to think about the séance and the medium. The library was dark when she entered. Moonlight was pouring in through one of the casement windows. She had the strangest feeling that there was another presence in the room besides her own.

"Father? Matilda?" she called softly into the darkness.

No one answered. Yet Julia sensed the presence of someone. She could almost hear their breathing. Everything was so still, so dark. Someone was there; she was sure of it.

She fumbled for the light switch and clicked it on. The room was bathed in a warm, cheery glow. She found that she had been quite mistaken. There was no one there.

The room was walled with books, floor to ceiling. Deep, comfortable reading chairs were spotted here and there, together with writing tables, a desk or two and deep, thick carpets to still any noise.

How she hoped to find any books on her ancestors among so huge a collection, she did not know. She started running her finger over the spines and saw at once that they were cataloged according to title. So, it did not take long to find the shelf that contained the volumes on the Cagliostro history. There were approximately thirteen volumes in all, printed in Latin, French, Italian, and two in German. The largest and most worn volume, she found, was an English publication. She pulled it from its resting place and carried it to one of the comfortable chairs dominated by a reading lamp with a tilted shade.

The first portion of the book dealt with the Cagliostros and the early popes of Rome. The sections of the tome were segregated into generations. Most of the reading was extremely uninteresting and rather laborious. Names fell upon names. There were Calgiostros in government, in art, in charitable works, in religion. Cagliostro women married other royal families, only to confuse the history all the more with different names.

She flipped over to the middle portion of the book and found that the volume turned, almost of its own accord, to a page which seemed more worn than the others. The spine of the book was broken at this point, she noticed, because the book fell flat in her lap.

The date was in May of 1789, she noted, and the name Lucius Cagliostro was underlined together with the name of his wife, Rosabella.

Julia settled herself deeper into the chair and began reading. She found she must have missed earlier references to Count Lucius Cagliostro, because this account began with saying that after he was expelled from his native city, Lucius and his wife, Rosabella, took up residence in the family estate outside of Rome, where the Italian authorities found him and accused him of many discreditable transactions such as fraud, forgery, and embezzlement. The most heinous charges against him were concerned with sorcery, however.

The authorities were put off, however, because the count's relatives—all very powerful and influential people—stood by him and received him with great kindness. The count, feeling secure, began entertaining people with his boasts of Satanic powers, and before long, had the inconceivable folly to put on an exhibition of these so-called Satanic powers before an assembly of select guests.

A detailed account of this exhibition was recorded by the Abate Benedetti, who mentioned all the notables present, which included a cardinal, a french ambassador, two princesses, the Marchese Vivaldi, Marchese Massimi, and a host of other Roman nobles.

The account went on to say that Count Cagliostro appeared before a makeshift altar wearing lavish raiment, gold-trimmed, lace-lined, with blood-red slippers on his feet. His robe was interwoven with odd cabalistic symbols and abstract designs. He was assisted by his wife, Rosabella, as well as other celebrants who were dressed similarly to himself. The altar was of black marble with tall golden candlesticks placed in a row. Above it hung a huge crucifix which was turned head downward.

The delegates present began drinking wine spiced with drugs of some description. They started to chant, beseeching the king of hell to appear to them. Several of the females present began ripping off their clothes until they stood stark naked before the altar.

Julia lowered her eyes until the shock had passed, then resumed reading.

A young calf was led in on a golden cord and the animal was sacrificed in the name of the Archfiend. The celebrants drank the blood and....

Julia found she could read no more and put the book aside. She kept thinking of the altar behind the statue of Anubis and how closely it resembled the description of the altar in the account; however, she did not remember seeing an inverted cross in the secret room.

She found herself picking up the book again. She read of another occasion on which Count Cagliostro appeared in black robes before an altar upon which a pile of skulls were placed. Atop the altar slab were stuffed monkeys and snakes, posed in attitudes to resemble their living counterparts. There were outlandish images of Indian, Chinese, Egyptian, Syrian, and

Persian idols and gods. Cagliostro's wife was beside him and together they entered into a trance. The count picked up a large crystal goblet and his wife filled it with clear spring water. He spoke strange words over the goblet and added to the water several drops of a liquid contained in a small bottle he carried on his person. He then proceeded to pour the liquid from the large glass goblet into smaller containers, and these he passed to those assembled. The water had been transformed into a deep, sparkling wine which proved delicious to the taste, it was claimed.

There were accounts of psychometry and crystal-gazing, of séances and fortune telling, of spells and charms and frightening orgies. Toward the end of the chapter, Julia read that the infamous Count Cagliostro was arrested while celebrating a mass to the Devil before a group of men and women, all of whom were naked. They were charged with breaking and entering a holy chapel and defiling the consecrated Host and the holy articles found therein.

Julia slammed the book shut and put it aside. Surely this was not the Count Cagliostro of whom her father was so proud? Yet, she could not help associating the account of the black mass with the room that lay hidden behind the statue of Anubis. The altar seemed similar in description. It was decked out with strange idols and gods.

She knew she should be revolted by the material she'd read, but something kept her from feeling appalled. After all, she told herself, it was more or less a part of what her father studied. He was interested in all kinds of people and their religions and beliefs, their cultures, their habits. The secret room was harmless enough, she decided.

She suddenly wanted to see that room again. Something was telling her to go there. She found herself standing and walking in the direction of the parlor. Once there, she went directly toward Anubis and touched the arm that held the royal staff. The panel slid back and Julia found herself standing before the strange altar with its row of tall, golden candlesticks. She didn't feel afraid, just fascinated without knowing why she should be fascinated. It suddenly all seemed very interesting.

After all, she reminded herself, there was nothing to be afraid of here; this was a part of her home. There was nothing that could harm her. The room was merely a display set up by her father as part of his hobby.

"Hello." Someone stepped from the shadows.

Julia gasped, covering her mouth with her hands.

"I didn't mean to frighten you," the man said. "But I suppose I did. I apologize."

Julia stared into the darkness. She raised a trembling hand and unconsciously found herself pointing a finger at the man. "I...you're...."

"I believe we met last evening," he said.

Julia stood, transfixed. His was the face she'd seen in the crystal ball in Madam Esperelda's tent. It was the very same face; she was positive of it.

"I'm quite real, you know," he said, stepping closer and flashing his fetching smile.

Finally she managed to say, "I didn't know what became of you. You disappeared before I got downstairs. I spoke to you, but you didn't seem to hear me."

"I heard you."

"But I didn't hear you," she argued.

"You'd just awakened from a nightmare; I doubt if you were fully awake when I spoke to you."

"Well, as long as we can hear each other now, I suppose we should introduce ourselves. I'm Julia Carson...no, I mean Julia Cagliostro."

"Yes, I know."

"What is your name?"

Again he shrugged. "Names aren't very important, but if you insist I have one, you may call me Adrian. If you do not care for that name, choose whatever name you like and I will answer to it."

He smiled at her with such warmth and tenderness that Julia

found her face getting red. "I've been expecting you," he said simply.

"You were in this room earlier," she found herself saying as her pulse began beating more rapidly.

"Yes. You came to replace the candlestick you dropped," he said.

"You knew that it was I who dropped it?"

"Who else? Your father would not have dropped it, and no one else is permitted to come here except accompanied by him."

"Then you mustn't tell him I stumbled upon this place," she said.

"And you must not tell him you talked with me."

"Why?"

"Because he will think of something for me to do and I do not feel much like working of late. I stay out of his way as much as possible."

"Is my father so hard a taskmaster?"

"Not at all, it is just that I am a very slothful individual."

Julia glanced around the room again. "This is a rather strange place for you to be hiding out."

"Strange? Why do you say that?"

"Well, surely it isn't the average kind of room one finds in a home."

"But this is not an average home, either. Your father is not an average person. Nor are you."

"Why did my father build this place? This room? Do you know?"

"He collected all these pieces on his travels. They were all things he found in various sites where Black Masses were supposed to have been celebrated."

"Black masses? You mean Satanic worship?"

"Yes. You've read your ancestor's history. Count Cagliostro was a very renowned man in such matters."

"But surely such practices are not carried on today?"

"There are those who are known to participate in such practices. Is it all so wrong in your eyes?"

"Of course, it's wrong."

"Why?"

She stammered a moment and then said, "Because it glorifies evil and defiles everything good and holy."

"But you must first decide what is evil and what is good," he said. "For some they are reversed, you know."

She gave a nervous little laugh. "You confuse me."

"I do not mean to. I am simply trying to show you that white is sometimes black and black is sometimes white." He broke off suddenly and laughed again. "But this is neither the time nor the place to launch into a lesson in theology or philosophy or ethics. It is late and I am keeping you from your bed. You must be tired after so long and hard a period of adjustment."

"Yes, I am a little tired," Julia admitted. "Will I see you again?"

"Undoubtedly. I am not a difficult fellow to find if you look hard enough."

Silently, quickly he stepped back into the shadows which seemed to swallow him up.

Julia stood there for a moment looking at the darkness into which he vanished, seemingly into thin air.

CHAPTER SIXTEEN

The mattress was old and sagged in the middle. Julia kept tossing about, trying to find a comfortable spot. She was only half asleep, thinking about the strange, attractive man whom she'd met in the secret room.

Adrian. Did he live here in the house? Where did he come from? What was he doing here? She thought of a hundred questions she wanted to ask him, and looked forward to their next meeting. He had been so charming and so attentive. She could picture his eyes, his smile. It was almost indecent, she thought, for a man to be so good-looking. Why had he been lurking in that strange room?

She snuggled deeper into the pillow. The secret room did not seem so frightening anymore, she decided.

Somewhere in the house a clock struck the midnight hour. She counted the strokes, hoping they'd help lull her to sleep. But immediately after the last stroke drifted into the stillness of the house, Julia's eyes flew open when she heard another sound...a sound which she'd heard before...just last night, in fact.

It was as if she were reliving the previous night. She listened to the horse's hooves approaching the house.

"Adrian," she said aloud. She sat up in bed. Her heart began to beat a little faster. Convinced that the horse could be no other than Adrian's, Julia quickly forgot about sleep and threw back the coverlet.

Outside, the moon was full and bright. The landscape was bathed in a silvery gray glow. Everything was muted and still except for the lone horseman who was trotting slowly toward the house. It was the same horse, the same rider, Julia saw to her happy surprise. It was Adrian sitting astride his white charger. Her pulse quickened.

At first she thought he was alone, but then she saw them. Walking quickly behind the horse was a small band of people. They were coming toward her. She watched as one by one they came up the path and went around the side of the house. As they passed under her window she recognized the Hastings brothers, her Aunt Rose, and several other men and women who had glanced at her when she walked to and from the inn.

It was an odd little procession. Everyone walked at the same pace and evenly spaced from one another. There was no hesitation or reluctance in their steps. They obviously knew where they were going and seemed anxious to get there.

Where were they going? Julia wondered. Adrian led them around to the side of the old house and they vanished from view. Wide awake now, Julia donned her slippers and pulled a robe around her. Her curiosity and anxiety to speak with Adrian again sent her hurrying out of her room. But, she didn't know where the people had gone. To the back of the house, surely, that was where they had been headed.

At the end of the corridor was a stairway, narrow and uncarpeted. She reached the bottom of the stairs and came face to face with a wood-paneled door, which was solidly locked. She jiggled the knob but to no avail.

She turned to start back up. However, on the dark landing she saw that there was still another doorway opening off onto another flight of stairs that led farther downward. She went down, thinking that she would wind up in the cellar.

Her head bumped a low-hanging light bulb whose cord trailed across her face, feeling like a thick cobweb. It sent a shiver up her spine. She yanked on the light and found herself standing in a gigantic room filled to overflowing with crates, boxes, and barrels of every size and description. Straw and sawdust was strewn everywhere. Half-unpacked cartons stood with their cardboard flaps up.

It was obviously her father's storeroom. She wandered through, turning and veering around the crates, angling around corners, dodging things that hung from overhead. She walked and gaped. Suddenly she looked back over her shoulder, and realized that she had lost sight of the stairway that had taken her down.

She stood, trying to figure out which way she'd come. Directly to her left she saw another flight of stairs, leading up. This stairway was draftier than the one she'd taken down. Her light robe and slippers were far from adequate in warding off the cold.

Halfway up, she thought she heard the sound of shuffling feet and low, murmuring voices. She stopped and strained to identify the sounds. She could not rightly tell in which part of the house she was located. She assumed she was somewhere under the front rooms, but she could not be positive of that. And the sounds were not coming from directly overhead. They seemed to be on the other side of the wall next to her. She pressed her ear to the partition and tried to listen, but all she heard was unidentified muffled voices and the shuffling of feet.

She went up, feeling the cold turning colder as she reached the top. She found herself again confronted by a door. This one, fortunately was unlocked.

A blast of cold night air hit at her the moment she swung the door open. Julia found herself staring out at shrubs and trees and the wide lawn that occupied the side area of the house. She stood there for a moment, shivering in her night clothes, trying to decide what she should do. Going back would accomplish little. Going outside would accomplish still less. But perhaps she might go around to the front and let herself into the house by that door. At least she would know where she was then.

She stepped outside, still trying to decide what she should do. Unconsciously she pulled the door shut. When she touched the knob, thinking she'd best go back and try to find the way she'd come, the knob wouldn't turn. The door was locked from the outside.

She stood shivering, knowing that she had no other alternative now but to try and gain entrance to the house through the front door. If that turned out to be locked, then she would just have to rouse someone inside. After all, she knew that there were people in there and they were not asleep.

The wind came up stronger as she hurried around the corner of the rambling old house. And with the wind came something else that chilled her. It sounded like the snarling of an animal. It was coming from somewhere near the bushes that skirted the woods far on the other side of the lawn. The moon was full and bright, and as she looked in the direction of the growl and she saw movement. Whatever it was was close to the ground and furry and four-legged. It was crouched, head down, tail tucked in, and was moving stealthily toward her.

Julia clutched the neck of her robe and pulled it tighter around her. She ducked into a shadow. She did not want to think of what kind of animal was prowling there. It was, undoubtedly, a wolf or something related to it—a wild dog, perhaps.

She pressed herself against the side of the house. Inch by inch, she moved slowly, silently alongside the house until she came to the wide front porch. She realized that once she stepped up on it, she would be in bright moonlight and easy prey for whatever was growling and threatening to attack.

A strange, gonglike sound came from inside the house. It vibrated with such force that the whole place seemed to tremble. Julia looked anxiously toward the beast creeping along the lawn. It had suddenly stopped, she saw. It settled itself back on its haunches and tilted back its head, gazing toward the moon. It started to howl, sending nerve-racking chills up and down Julia's spine.

With the beast distracted, she felt she could rush to the door and safety before it reached her. Quickly she went up on the porch, ran to the front door and pushed down on the latch.

The door was unlocked.

She let herself in, slamming the door shut behind her. She

leaned against it, getting her breathing back to normal. After a few minutes she turned and parted the lace curtains that covered the door's glass panel. She peeked out and saw that the beast was gone. The lawn was empty.

Had she imagined a growling beast? No, surely not. She'd seen it quite clearly; she'd heard it. It had been real enough.

She moved away from the door and started toward the staircase. Then again she heard the strange chanting sounds. They seemed to be coming from somewhere near the parlor. She went toward it and found the darkened room quite empty. Still, the sounds of chanting people drifted on the air. She walked quietly into the center of the room and tried to pinpoint from where the sounds came.

She realized after a moment that the chanting was coming from behind the paneled wall guarded by Anubis. They were in the secret room. Adrian had led his little following into the house, and they had collected together in that strange room with its icons and black hangings, its strange paintings, and imposing, black altar.

Thoughts of what she'd read about Count Cagliostro flashed across her mind and she found herself trembling. Surely there was not a gathering for that purpose here in this house. What had she stumbled upon? She had seen the townspeople come toward the house, and now she was sure that they were inside, in that secret room.

But why? For what purpose? Did they really perform Satanic rituals similar to the ones she'd read about? Were they conjuring up the powers of hell? Surely not.

A light moved past the doorway that led to the entrance hall. Someone was walking about, candle in hand. She stood quite still in the dark room, hoping she would not be discovered prowling about.

Suddenly the chanting coming from beyond the paneling grew louder and more insistent. She could not help but hear. They were all chanting in Latin. She started translating the words, as once she did during the séance. This Latin was more formal than that used by the medium; Julia had less difficulty with the translation.

"We are pleased and contented with thee, O great Prince. We want thee in peace. Go from us in quiet and without trouble or stay, and we will revel and feast with you in your name. Do not forsake us, O great and mighty Lord."

Over and over this was repeated until Julia found the words falling softly, comfortably on her ears. She did not know their significance; it was just that they were soft and enchanting to hear. She began to feel a part of the words. She felt herself getting lighter, more buoyant. She wasn't conscious that her feet were still touching the floor. She felt herself raised from the carpet. Again and again the words entranced her until she found herself walking, almost blindly, toward the statue of Anubis.

"We are pleased and contented with thee, O great Prince. We want thee in peace. Go from us in quiet and without trouble or stay and we will revel and feast with you in your name. Do not forsake us, O great and mighty Lord."

She took another step forward and found herself directly before Anubis. She looked up into the yellow, piercing eyes. The hideous head seemed no longer hideous. She wanted to go into the secret room and join the throng assembled on the other side of the wall. She wanted to see the lighted candles, the robed celebrants. She wanted to see *Him*.

Julia reached out to touch the arm that held the royal staff.

"No," a voice said sharply. It came from directly behind her.

At first Julia wasn't sure she had heard anyone speak. She reached for the arm that held the golden staff. Someone wrenched her arm down and turned her sharply.

"You are sleep-walking, child," Matilda said kindly. "Go back to your bed. Your time is not yet come. You must not appear until all is ready for you."

Blindly Julia let herself be taken by the arm and led away. She was unaware of where or who she was, or where she was going.

CHAPTER SEVENTEEN

Julia awoke happy and eager to start her day. The sun poured in through the windows, bathing the room with a golden glow. She wanted to be up and about; there was so much to be done. And the first thing on her agenda would be a new mattress, she told herself as she stretched and yawned. She wondered idly if Adrian might be available to help her with some of the work that had to be done.

Matilda came in with a breakfast tray. "Don't get the notion that I'll be making a habit of serving you breakfast in bed," she said, pretending to be annoyed.

"Oh, Matilda, you shouldn't have."

"I know I shouldn't. It was his orders," she said, tossing her head in the direction of the door. "He said you've got to be spoiled, it being your first morning here and all."

"I'm famished," Julia said as Matilda settled the tray in front of her.

"You look well rested for someone who was gallivanting around most of the night," the old woman said.

Julia laughed. "How did you know I was gallivanting around?"

"Don't you remember me shooing you off to bed when I found you in the parlor?"

Julia had poured herself a cup of coffee. The cup paused between lip and saucer. "No," she said as she frowned at the old woman. "Did you find me in the parlor?"

Matilda nodded gravely.

"That's strange," Julia said, thinking hard about the events of last night. "I remember going there to investigate the noises, but I don't remember you being there."

"I don't know what you were doing. I found you standing in the middle of the room, like you were sound asleep on your feet. You were listening to something, by the look of you, but I don't know what you might have been listening to. I didn't hear anything."

"There were people in the house."

"People?"

"Yes. I saw Adrian leading a group of people from Belham into the house sometime after midnight. I heard them chanting and moving around. I went to investigate and got myself lost. Luckily the front door was open, because I managed to get outside somehow and I came in through the front door."

"You were dreaming, child. First of all, there was no one here in the house last night. Second, the front door is always locked. *Always.* Third, who is this Adrian you said you saw?"

"Adrian? He's the man on horseback who came to me at the inn night before last. He said he works for my father. My father told me all about him."

"Oh, *him*," Matilda said. She looked slightly uncomfortable.

"Surely you know Adrian?"

The old woman nodded. "I know him. I just forgot for a moment. He comes and he goes. I forget he's around."

"But surely I just didn't dream all those things. I was wide awake when I heard Adrian ride up with the people following him. I saw them with my own eyes. They came just after the clock struck midnight. They entered the house somewhere on the side or at the back. I wasn't dreaming, Matilda. I saw them. They were quite real, believe me." She thought for a moment. "There was my Aunt Rose and the Hastings brothers and...."

"Well, if you say they were real, then they were real. But I neither saw nor heard anyone. You were dreaming. When I found you, you were walking in your sleep."

Julia smiled. The old woman had obviously not heard the

people who had gathered in the secret room. She wondered if her father knew that they'd come here last night. Adrian knew, of course. Strange, how she couldn't remember anything after seeing the beast outside and rushing back into the house. She vaguely remembered going into the parlor and then everything got hazy. Matilda said she'd found her and led her back to bed. She didn't remember that at all.

Had she dreamed the whole thing?

No, the people had been real enough. She saw them and heard them.

Or had she?

Her father hadn't heard the people either. He knew nothing about Adrian's bringing them here. He told her he would speak to Adrian if he could. "Unfortunately," her father said, "Adrian went away and it is difficult to say when he'll be back."

"Adrian gone? Oh, no. I so wanted him to help with some of the heavy work."

"Heavy work?"

"Matilda and I can hardly manage moving the furniture around, besides the rest of the strenuous work that needs to be done here."

"Well, Adrian doesn't have to be here to have that done. Any man in Belham who is available will gladly help you. Go get as many as you need. All you have to do is ask. They'll come."

Julia was disappointed about Adrian being gone, but she didn't brood on it for very long. There was so much that needed doing. Before long she found she had almost forgotten about the dashingly handsome Adrian, and had lost herself completely in redoing her room and several other rooms, while she was at it.

The days passed quickly and with each passing day, she found herself more and more in love with her father. She wanted to be at his side always. She was truly happy for the first time in her life. She never thought life could be so wonderful.

Her days were perfect. She could not say as much for her nights, however, because they confused her. She slept well enough, but it seemed that she was plagued by the strangest dreams—only they weren't really dreams, she felt. They were as real as when she saw Adrian bringing the townspeople to the house, and going in search of them, only to be found walking in her sleep. Almost every night something similar would occur. She would hear noises, see people and wander through the house, only to find herself back in her bed without having accomplished anything.

One night she heard Adrian's magnificent stallion gallop up and come to stand directly beneath her window. The horse whinnied and neighed. She found herself getting out of bed and going out to it. She mounted the fiery steed and galloped off over the meadows and the fields. She knew it had to be a dream for she'd never ridden a horse before. Yet in the morning when she awoke, her limbs and body ached as though she actually had ridden the stallion through the night.

She mentioned these strange dreams—or were they night-mares—to her father and also to Matilda.

Her father said, "You're working yourself too hard. Don't overtire yourself so much and these dreams you're having will go away soon enough."

"But they are so weird, Father," Julia said. "One night I dreamed that I went out of the house and walked into the woods. I pricked my finger on a thorn bush. In the morning there was a spot of blood on my pillow and my finger bore a cut."

"It means nothing, child. You most likely cut your finger while you slept. A sharp button, an open pin, anything might have jabbed your finger during the night."

"But there were other things."

"Now, now," her father cautioned. "Do not fret over these dreams of yours. They are harmless enough."

Julia tried not to dwell on her dreams, but the dreams were becoming more and more terrifying. Each night something new and more bizarre occurred. It was getting so that she was afraid to close her eyes. She never had trouble falling into a deep sleep the minute her head touched the pillow, even when she fought desperately against sleep.

* * * * * *

The clock at the top of the stairs had finished striking the eleventh hour. Julia sat at her dressing table putting the final strokes to her hair. The day had been wonderful, as usual, and she was anxious for a good night's sleep. She turned back the coverlet but before slipping under it, she crossed the hall and tapped on her father's door.

"I know you will think I'm being foolish, Father," she said when he answered her knock, "but would you be an angel and lock me in my room. I'm convinced I've been roaming about in my sleep. If you'll lock me in, I won't be able to wander too far."

Her father laughed and tried to convince her that she was indeed being foolish, but in the end he agreed.

Julia went back into her room. Her father kissed her goodnight, tucked her into her bed, and then locked her door, taking the key with him. He said he'd unlock the door the moment he awoke the following morning, which would be long before Julia awoke.

She felt better. She snuggled into the comfort of the new mattress and let her eyelids droop closed. Let the dreams come, she thought. She was safe and secure in her room.

It was after midnight when she heard the voice of a child calling to her. She was sure it was little Meg's voice she heard. It seemed to be coming from somewhere outside the house. Julia opened her eyes. She hadn't dreamed the voice. It was real. She heard it again. She thought it was calling her name.

She got out of bed and went to the window. There was no one outside.

But she knew there was a child out there somewhere, crying, needing her comfort. Without realizing what she was doing, Julia found herself donning her clothes. She took her light coat from the closet and put it around her. She went to the door. Something inside her warned her that the door would be locked and that she had dressed for nothing.

The door was not locked. The knob turned easily in her hand

and the door swung open.

She closed the door to her room carefully, to be sure not to disturb the others in the house. She went along the hallway and down the curved staircase. The door leading outside was also unlocked, she found. But Matilda had said the front door was never unlocked. She went out into the night. She did not know exactly where she was going, but she knew she must find the child who was crying and bring it back to her father's house where it would be safe.

The first cottage she came across was unlighted. Julia boldly tried the door. It was bolted from the inside. She went around the cottage, peering into the windows. An elderly couple slept in the only bedroom, but there was no child.

* * * * * * *

She continued down the road, walking like a woman possessed. Cottage after cottage she inspected and tried to gain entrance; all were dark, however, and all were locked against her.

At the end of the lane she saw a trail of lazy smoke curling from a chimney. She went through the gate and up the flower-edged walk. There were no lights on in the cottage. Everyone was asleep. When she tried the latch, the door opened easily and silently. Julia pushed at the door and cautiously stepped into the snug little room. The fire was almost burned out. The house was hushed and still. She walked carefully across the braided rugs.

She stopped suddenly when she caught her reflection in a mirror near a doorway. What was she doing here? Where was she? She saw her face in the glass and yet it wasn't her face; it was another's.

She turned quickly away, intent upon rushing out of the cottage and seeking the safety and comfort of her own room, her own home.

Then she heard the child's voice again. It called her name. Yes, it was Julia the child wanted. It was unhappy and wanted to be with Julia. It was little Meg. It had to be Meg who was calling to her. Someone had adopted little Meg and had brought her here to Belham. They were mistreating the child. She'd have to steal Meg away.

Stealthily Julia crept through the cottage until she found the room she was looking for. A small child, a lovely little girl, lay sleeping soundly in her tiny bed. She wore her hair tied with yellow hair ribbons which matched the yellow of her lovely little lace nightdress.

The child did not stir when Julia picked her up. The little girl would be safe once she got her home, Julia told herself as she gathered up a blanket and wrapped the girl in it to keep her sheltered from the cold of the night. Quietly, carefully she picked her way back out of the cottage, closing the door softly behind her.

Somewhere behind her she thought she heard someone crying.

Julia went quickly along the road, cradling the little girl to keep her warm. She went as quickly as possible and finally saw her father's house looming up before her. The child was heavy. Julia's arms ached from the weight of the girl and the long walk. She hurried on until she was back inside the house. Without hesitating, she carried the child up the curved staircase. She went into her room and laid the child in her bed.

"No, not here," a voice said. Julia turned sharply and found Adrian standing in the doorway. "The child was not meant to be brought up here, Julia."

"Adrian? I've missed you," she said.

"Give me the child, Julia. She does not belong to you."

Julia stood motionless, helpless. Every ounce of strength seemed to have been sapped from her body. She stood watching Adrian lift the child in his arms and start out of the room. Numbly, Julia followed after him. They went back down the stairs and into the parlor. Adrian touched the arm of Anubis and the wall slid open. Together they entered the secret room. Adrian walked directly to the altar and laid the child down atop the marble slab.

"She will be safe here with me, Julia," he told her.

"But she needs me."

"Go to bed, Julia. Your work is finished."

She did as he said, returning to her room where she fell into bed without removing her coat or dress. She had never felt so tired. Her eyes closed and she drifted into a deep, deep sleep.

She awoke to the sound of birds chirping merrily outside her window ledge. She sat bolt upright in the bed, remembering what had transpired during the night, but when she looked down at herself, she saw that she was dressed in the nightgown she'd put on before retiring. She glanced at the door to her room. She rushed over to it and tried the knob. The door was locked.

Panic struck her. "Father, Father," she yelled, pounding on the door.

A moment later she heard the key being turned from the other side. The door opened. Julia threw herself into her father's arms.

"Oh, Julia. I'm so sorry," her father said. "I overslept, which is most unusual. I was sure I'd be up long before you."

Julia stared up at him through her frightened tears. "Was my door locked all night long?"

"Of course, child. Why do you ask?"

She turned from him. "Then it was just a dream," she said with a sigh. "Just a dream."

"What was a dream, child?"

"It was a dream," she repeated. She dropped herself down onto the side of her bed. "Only a dream."

Out of the corner of her eye she saw a child's yellow hair ribbon lying on the floor next to the bed.

CHAPTER EIGHTEEN

"What is it, Julia?" her father asked as he watched her try to fight back her panic. "What's wrong?"

Julia couldn't speak. She pointed to the hair ribbon.

"It's just a ribbon," her father said, picking it up. "What is there to be so afraid of?"

"It belongs to a child from the village. I kidnapped her last night." She felt sick to her stomach. She wanted to die.

Her father laughed. "It's true. I kidnapped a small girl last night. I thought it was little Meg."

Her father sat down beside her and gathered her into his arms. "Now, how is that possible, Julia? You had another of your bad dreams, I suspect."

"No, it couldn't have been a dream. The little girl was wearing yellow hair ribbons exactly like this one when I carried her from her bed. Oh, father, her parents must be frantic. We must find her and return her to them." She found herself clutching at him.

"Julia, calm yourself. You dreamed again. You couldn't possibly have kidnapped a child. You were locked in your room, remember. I had the only key."

Julia ran her hands through her hair. She tried to think straight. It was true that the door had been locked when she went to bed and it was still locked when she awoke. But the hair ribbon? It wasn't hers. Where did it come from?

"Now, listen," her father said. "If a child was taken from her bed in the middle of the night, surely her parents would be out searching for it. Now, to satisfy you, we'll go into the town and ask if anyone is missing their child. I'm sure you'll find that no little child is missing."

"But a little girl *is* missing. I carried her here and gave her to Adrian who took her to—" She cut herself off.

Her father laughed again and shook his head. "We'll just have to do something about these dreams of yours. They are becoming more fanciful each time. Come. Get dressed. We will have a nice hot breakfast, and then we'll walk into Belham to dispel your fears and prove that you aren't a kidnapper."

* * * * * * *

Julia felt much better after their visit in Belham. No child was reported missing. She took her father to the very cottage she had dreamed she visited. The young couple did have a little girl; her grandparents had just stopped by to take the child on a picnic. And yes, the child did have yellow hair ribbons, but she lost one of them one day while out playing. They believed it was lost out near Dr. Cagliostro's house.

"See," said her father when they arrived back home. "You just imagined the whole thing."

"I suppose you're right," Julia admitted. "But that young couple acted strangely, I thought."

"Strangely? How so?"

"The wife. She seemed very nervous or afraid."

"Oh, Julia. You do have a habit of imagining things. They seemed perfectly normal to me."

Julia smiled and kissed his cheek. "I guess you're right. I am being somewhat of a bother, aren't I?"

* * * * * * *

She was almost afraid to go to bed that night. Again she asked her father to lock her in her room just on the chance that she might again walk in her sleep.

It started the moment she closed her eyes. She found herself being lifted up by a heavy, black mist. It was all around her, blinding her, choking her. Then the mist cleared and she was standing on a lonely road in the middle of an immense, open plain. Far in the distance was a light burning in the window of a stone house with a thatched roof. She began walking toward it. Her feet didn't seem to touch the ground. The wind rushed past her ears. The sky overhead was strewn with threatening dark clouds.

It took no time at all to reach the little house and just as she entered the gate, a heavy splatter of rain began to fall. She hurried up the path and into the house. A young boy—no more than thirteen or fourteen years of age—was sitting before a fire, reading a book. He had chestnut-brown hair and large clear eyes of the same color. She stood smiling down at him.

The boy looked up in surprise when he heard the door open and close and saw Julia come into the room.

"Hello," the boy said as he set aside his book. "Is that rain I hear? Did you want shelter?"

She gazed into his face. Her eyes sent out a bright, yellowish gleam. She stared deep into his eyes until she felt them lock firmly on her own. She reached out and touched his temples. She ran her hand through his hair, all the while keeping her eyes fixed solidly on his. Neither of them spoke. She pressed her fingers hard against his temples and felt his pulse under her touch. Then she moved her hand over the top of his head and made tiny circles and squares. She began tracing strange patterns on the top of his skull. The boy's shoulders sagged and he fell asleep.

"Did I hear somebody come in, Danny?" a man called as he entered through a door toward the rear of the little house. Seeing Julia standing there he stood still.

"Who are you?" He looked from Julia to his young brother who stood transfixed before her. "What are you doing?"

Julia turned suddenly and ran out the door, out into the pouring rain. She heard the man come after her but he did not follow her. He called, but Julia ran as fast as she could.

She awoke the next morning and found her nightclothes soaked, as though she really had been running in a downpour. But the door to her room was locked as she had expected. Her hair lay dank and straight. Her feet were stained with mud.

Again she pounded on the door, calling for her father.

"I must be getting senile," he said after unlocking the door. "I'd forgotten I'd locked you in again last night." He looked at her. "Julia, your clothes are damp. What were you doing?"

She told him of her newest dream. She was shaking with fear. She didn't know what it all meant.

"But it didn't rain last night. The ground is as dry as powder."

"Then how do you explain the mud on my feet and my wet hair?"

He shook his head. "I don't know, Julia. Perhaps someone is playing a joke."

"A joke? Who would do such a thing? You are the only one with the key to my room. Surely you didn't do anything so foolish as to dampen my nightclothes and smear mud on my feet."

"Hardly, child. But there must be a logical explanation. Come, get yourself bathed and dressed. Matilda is putting breakfast on the table."

Julia tried to think of some logical explanation all the while she soaked in the tub, but none came to her.

And what had the dream meant? It seemed a harmless excursion, if that indeed was what it had been—an excursion. She'd walked into someone's house and laid her hands on a young boy's head. What did it mean?

Finished dressing, she started down the stairs. She heard angry voices coming from the direction of her father's study. The door stood partly open. There was a man standing with his back to her. The shape of him looked familiar. He was shouting at her father, shouting quite loudly.

"I demand to know what you did to my brother!" he yelled.

"I don't know what you are talking about," her father answered.

Julia pushed the door open and the hinge squeaked. The man turned. She stared at him. He was the same man she'd seen in her dream, the man who'd chased her away. There was no mistake about it. It was the same fair hair, the same fine face, chiseled chin, rugged features. It was the same man.

"It was you," the man said, pointing an accusing finger at her.

Julia fled to the safety of her room. She slammed the door shut and threw herself across the bed. Her fear and her frustration caused her to burst into a flood of tears.

There was no mistaking the man. He was the same one who had been in her dream. It had been his house she was in last night. But how did she get there? And what had she done to the young boy? His brother, he'd told her father. It had been his brother whom Julia had touched. But why? Why had she gone to the house and stood silently before the lad? Why had she pressed her fingers into his temples and stroked his hair and made those weird patterns on his skull? It made no sense. Yet the man downstairs had recognized her, and she had recognized him.

She had to talk to him. She had to find out if in fact she had visited his house during the night. But she could not do it in the presence of her father. Her father would not want her to get mixed up with so irate a man. She frowned when she thought about her father and his reaction to her dreams. He didn't seem to want to discuss them. It was as if he discouraged her even talking to him about them.

Julia raised herself up and went back out into the corridor. She walked the length of it and went down the dark, uncarpeted stairs that led toward the back of the house. The door at the bottom landing was unlocked this time. She opened it and found herself in a large pantry.

From there she found the kitchen. There was no one about. Matilda was obviously in the dining room. Julia skirted the large, square table and let herself out the back door. She went around the house and waited on the porch until the man came out.

He was still too angry even to notice her there. He went down the steps and walked angrily toward a late-model car which stood in the road.

"Wait," Julia called softly.

The man turned.

"May I speak with you, please?" she said.

"You bet you can," he said, grabbing her arm and pulling her roughly toward his automobile. "You were the one who came to my house last night. What did you do to my brother?"

"Please, you're hurting me." she tried to pry his fingers from her arm.

"I'll do more than hurt you if you don't tell me what kind of a spell you put on my kid brother."

"Spell? I don't know what you're talking about."

He opened the door of the car with his free hand and pushed Julia down onto the seat. He stood outside, looking down at her.

"Now, I want some answers," he said angrily.

"Please, you must let me explain," Julia pleaded. "I don't know what you're talking about. I do remember seeing you last night, but it was in a dream I had."

"A dream, huh? Now that's what I call a very convenient excuse...but not a very likely story. Surely you can come up with something a little better than that."

"Please, you must believe me. I've been having the wildest, the strangest dreams of late. I've tried to convince my father that they were more than just dreams, but he won't listen to me. He thinks I'm just imagining it all. But you must believe me. I'm frightened. I'm afraid I'm doing things, things that are wrong, but I'm asleep when I'm doing them and I can't help myself."

The man's expression softened somewhat. "You mean you're not conscious?"

"Tell me about your brother," Julia said. "I dreamed last night that I went to a small stone house with a thatched roof."

"That sounds like my place," he said.

"It started to rain. Something told me to let myself into your house. I went in and stood there gazing at a young boy, thirteen or fourteen years old, sitting in front of a fire, reading a book."

"That was Danny, my brother. You'd come in out of the rain. I heard you."

Julia frowned. "But my father said it didn't rain last night. He said the ground was as dry as powder."

"Your father? I didn't know Cagliostro had a daughter."

"I just recently arrived. My parents and I became separated when I was a baby. I managed to find Father and I live with him now. But tell me more about your brother. I really don't remember doing anything to him but looking at him. I pressed his temples and touched his head. Other than that, I did nothing wrong."

"Nothing wrong? You bewitched him, that's what you did to him!"

"Bewitched him? No. How is that possible? I don't know how to bewitch anybody."

"You are Cagliostro's flesh and blood aren't you? Surely you are not so blind as not to see or know what goes on in that house of yours." He looked at her for a moment, seeing the innocence shine from her face. "Even if you really did arrive here but a few days ago, surely you know what kind of a house you're living in."

Julia glanced toward her father's house. "What do you mean? Nothing goes on here. I live there with my father and Matilda, the housekeeper."

The man frowned down at her. "You arrived just recently? Is that what you said?"

"Yes. I lived and worked in New York until just a week or so ago. I'd been trying to find my parents ever since I can remember. When I finally did, I moved here to be with him. My mother is dead, I was told."

"Then you don't know about Cagliostro and this town?"

"Know? What is there to know?"

The man gave her an exasperated look. He felt he didn't believe her, yet something in her face said she was telling the truth. He wondered how many other innocent young girls the evil Cagliostro had lured here under all sorts of pretenses. Was this another of his victims, or was she truly his flesh and blood, his real live daughter?

There was the sudden sound of a door opening and slamming shut. Julia and the man looked toward the house. Dr. Cagliostro was standing on the porch, hands on hips. He had an angry scowl on his face. He started down the steps.

"Leave my daughter alone," he shouted to the man. "Get off my property, Dunston, or I'll run you off. You've no business trying to make trouble here. Take your complaints elsewhere."

"Look," the stranger said hurriedly, "I have to talk with you. Can you meet me later? There's an old abandoned church at the far end of town. I'll meet you there at noontime today."

He stepped back, helping Julia out of the car. And turned to confront Julia's father.

"I'll leave now," he said. "But don't think I won't be back. And you will have plenty of explaining to do. Whatever kind of spell you put on Danny had better be lifted, and damn quick."

"Get off my property, Dunston. I know nothing about your brother or any spell."

"No, but your daughter does. Ask her."

Dr. Cagliostro put his arm around Julia and pulled her against him. "I suggest you leave, Dunston. I'll not warn you again. If you persist in these wild accusations, I'm afraid I won't be responsible for what might happen to you."

"I'm not afraid of you, Cagliostro. I know how to handle your kind. You can't frighten me away. I've come to deal with you and that is exactly what I intend doing."

"Get out."

"I'm going. But as I said, I'll come back. And when I do, you'd better beware."

CHAPTER NINETEEN

The man—Dunston—had said she had cast a spell on his brother.

But that was utterly impossible. She knew nothing about charms or spells.

And I promised to meet him, Julia told herself as she let her father lead her back into the house. Why had she agreed to meet him? Surely he wasn't serious when he accused her and her father of being responsible for casting spells.

"I hope he didn't upset you, my dear," her father said. "He is the new doctor I mentioned. I never thought he would be so strange a man."

"What did it all mean?" Julia asked.

"He had some insane notion that I—or you—cast a spell on his younger brother. He most likely read the old Cagliostro stories and heard I lived here in the same town. This is the sort of thing that used to crop up constantly. That is why my father changed our name when we moved to this country. I see people do not change, and they never seem to forget."

"I saw that man last night, Father, in my dream. I was in his house. I met his younger brother."

"You *dreamed* you saw that man last night. You *dreamed* you were in his house. You *dreamed* you met his brother. You dreamed all of it, Julia. None of it actually happened."

"But he recognized me also. He said I was in his house and that I put a spell on his brother."

"I'll have no more talk of Dunston and his insane ravings.

He and his brother were staying at the inn the night you lodged there. You most likely saw them and dreamed about them. The subconscious mind is a very tricky fellow. You could well have seen them and not realized it."

"But Father—"

"No, no more, Julia. Please. Dunston managed to upset me quite enough. Come. Let's have our breakfast and try to settle ourselves and forget all about dreams and madmen like Dunston."

They ate, almost in silence, each consumed by his own secret thoughts. Dunston had very obviously upset him, Julia thought as she watched her father pick at his food. She couldn't help but wonder why her father kept avoiding the obvious possibility that her dreams were much more than dreams. She hadn't seen Dunston or his brother at Aunt Rose's inn. Besides, Aunt Rose said she never took in lodgers, especially strangers, and Dunston, according to her father, was new in Belham.

She hadn't intended keeping the rendezvous with Dunston, but suddenly she found herself looking at things differently. Her father refused to discuss her dreams. She had to talk about them to someone. Dunston was a doctor. Perhaps he would be able to help her.

The morning dragged. Dr. Cagliostro closeted himself in his study. Julia tried to take an interest in the new paint and drapery samples, but her mind wasn't on decorating. She glanced at the clock a thousand times, trying to find some excuse to get out of the house and into Belham.

"Oh, dear," Julia said as she dropped some fabrics over a chair. "Today was the day I promised Aunt Rose I'd stop in and visit."

Matilda looked up from her work. "Your Aunt Rose? I didn't think you had spoken to her since you came here."

"I ran into her the other day when father and I were in town," she lied. "She invited me to visit. I might just as well join her for lunch and it will save you the bother, Matilda."

The old woman grunted and went on with whatever it was

she was doing.

Julia left the house without even bothering to change her dress. She was early, but simply to justify her lie, she decided to stop at the inn and visit with Aunt Rose for a few minutes.

Aunt Rose was surprised when Julia walked through the front door. "I thought the old house swallowed you up for good," she said as she kissed the girl's cheek. "I get all the reports about how hard you're working." She laid a finger alongside her cheek and studied Julia's face for a moment. "You look tired, Julia. Your father's working you too hard."

Julia shook her head. "No, it isn't his fault. I just haven't been sleeping as soundly as I'd like. I'm still in the throes of getting used to the change in my living habits," she said. "I'll adjust soon enough."

Her Aunt regarded her for a moment longer, then smiled. "Of course you will. Come along, I'll fix you a bit of lunch."

"No, thank you, Aunt Rose. I can't stay but a few minutes. I just came in to shop at the general store. I need some thread and things. Oh, and by the way, I met a man at the house this morning who father said is new in Belham. His name is Dunston, I believe. He is a doctor or something."

"Oh, yes. Jason Dunston. Yep, he's a doctor all right. He has a younger brother, Danny, I think the boy's name is. What was Dunston doing at your father's house?"

"Just stopped to speak with father about something. I saw him and he looked very familiar. I told my father that I thought I'd met him before. He said it was possible that I'd seen him here, that he and his brother were staying here the night I arrived."

"Nope, they never stayed here." Suddenly Aunt Rose bit her tongue. "Your father said that, huh? Well, now that I think of it, I do believe they did ask to stay a day or two recently. They rented old Mr. Hastings place and the roof was leaking or some such thing, and they wanted me to put them up for a night or two."

"Oh, then, that explains it. I most likely caught a glimpse of them and didn't remember."

"That's possible," her aunt agreed.

"Well, I should be off," Julia said, glancing at her watch. "There is so much to be done. You will have to come up and see all Matilda and I have accomplished with the old place. It's beginning to look like a house, instead of an aging relic. But come at a decent hour when I can show you around, not after midnight."

"What do you mean by that?"

"I noticed you following Adrian to the house the other night. I went down—"

Aunt Rose cut her off with, "Adrian? Who's Adrian?"

Why did everyone ask that same question whenever she mentioned Adrian's name. Matilda had done the same thing. "Adrian. You know. The man who works for my father."

"Oh, him."

Matilda had said that too, Julia remembered.

"I didn't come to the house the other night," her aunt said.

"Of course you did. I saw you. I went downstairs to meet you all, but I got lost in the house."

"You must have been dreaming, girl. I haven't set foot in that house of yours since I don't know when."

Julia forced herself to smile. "Maybe you're right. I have been pestered by strange dreams of late. Oh, well. I should be off. There is so much to be done."

"Don't be a stranger, now. Come when we can have more time to chat. There is so much I want to tell you."

Julia stopped at the general store, even though it was after twelve, and bought a few notions. She tucked them into her handbag and strolled leisurely toward the old abandoned church she'd seen when she first arrived in Belham.

Suddenly she wondered why the only church in Belham was abandoned? It hadn't occurred to her before. Now it looked like a derelict ship adrift on a dead sea.

Dunston was nowhere to be seen when she entered the rear of the church. The inside, she found, was as she had expected: dusty, neglected, and murky. There was something about the atmosphere of the place that bristled the hairs on the back of her neck.

Julia walked slowly down the center aisle. She had her back to the altar niche, but something made her turn and look at it. She felt a stab of fear as she looked at the stripped altar. There was nothing to be afraid of, she told herself, yet she was afraid nonetheless. She took an involuntary step backward, then another.

What was frightening her? She felt compelled to keep her eyes averted from the little niche. What was there to be afraid of? She'd been in churches and chapels in the past and never felt like this.

She forced herself to look directly at the altar niche. Her eyes widened with fright again and she covered her face with her hands. What was it? What was frightening her so? There was nothing on the altar; it was stripped bare. There were no statues or figures or shapes to scare or alarm her. Yet she continued to keep her eyes averted for fear of whatever it was that was there, frightening her.

She heard a door open and looked around. The man, Dunston, stood in the doorway that led to a small room. He motioned to her. Wanting to get away from the altar niche, Julia rushed to him.

Once inside the room, she closed the door and leaned against it. She found she was breathing heavily. Dunston studied her for a moment. He had an odd expression on his face. His eyes too had a strange look about them.

"I just did not think," he said.

"What? What do you mean?" Julia asked with a frown.

He waved the remark aside. "Never mind. Are you all right now?"

"Yes. I don't know what came over me. There was something out there that frightened the wits out of me. But there was nothing there."

"Just the stained-glass window behind the altar," he said. "Come." He took her hand and led her to a straight-backed chair that sat in the center of the room. He dusted the seat with his handkerchief and sat her down.

"I think we'd better start at the beginning," he said. "I'm sure I did the right thing by asking you to meet me here, and now that I see what happened, I'm convinced of it."

"You're making no sense. What do you mean, 'what happened'? I don't understand."

"You said something out there scared you. And you don't know why you were frightened?"

"No, I don't."

"Can't you guess?"

"Guess what?"

He shook his head. "Then you really don't know about your father and this town of Belham."

"Will you please make sense. First you're asking me to guess why I'm afraid of the inside of an old, abandoned church, and then you imply that there is something amiss in Belham and with my father."

"Something amiss?" He threw back his head and laughed.

Julia stared at him. He was as mad as her father claimed him to be.

He must have read her mind. "You believe me mad, I suppose." He shook his head as though to shake off an unpleasant thought. "I might well be mad, for all I know. Ever since I got mixed up in this Cagliostro business, I find it harder and harder to believe the cruelty and the insanity that is going on."

"What Cagliostro business?" Julia demanded. "You are speaking of my family."

Dunston sighed. "Have you always known you were Cagliostro's daughter?"

"No," she answered, surprised at his question. "I knew my mother was Bridget Bishop. I was brought up in an orphanage. They said my father was unknown."

"Bridget Bishop. Then you didn't know about the Cagliostro family until you came here?"

"My father told me his real name was Cagliostro and not Bishop. He gave me a book to read. I'm familiar somewhat now with my ancestors."

"And you read about the infamous Count Cagliostro?"

"Yes. My father laughed about him. He said he was the worst of the lot. What I read about him I did not particularly enjoy, but that was centuries ago."

"And you don't think anyone practices those arts anymore?"

"Surely not. This is the twentieth century. Everyone knows that such things are utter nonsense."

Dunston gazed at her for a moment and then started pacing back and forth in front of her. "Years ago I graduated from medical school convinced that a doctor was the only person who could make the lame walk, the blind see, the sick well. I learned over the years, however, that actually it isn't the doctor and it isn't the medicine that cures. It is the mind. A pill won't stop pain unless the taker of that pill, in his mind, has faith in the power of the pill. It isn't the pill's strength really that does the work, it is the mind power that cures the pain."

Julia watched him as he went back and forth, back and forth. She was trying to understand what he was getting at.

"I became interested in the workings of the mind and took up studies in psychiatry. From there I moved into the realms of the various religious beliefs, because religion is nothing more than a state of mind. It was during my research of religions that I stumbled upon a group of Satanists—people who worship the Devil."

Julia opened her mouth to say something, but he waved her to be still a moment longer.

"I was married at the time to a lovely young thing." He smiled at Julia. "You remind me a great deal of Nancy, my wife." He turned his head quickly and cleared his throat. "Nancy fell under the spell of these Satan worshipers. I, of course, was convinced that it was a bunch of hogwash, but Nancy firmly believed that through the right kind of concentration, Lucifer could be conjured up.

"I refused to get too deeply involved with the Satanists and I ordered Nancy to stay away from them. But she was meeting with them in secret. I didn't know anything about it. Then one day she disappeared. They found her body several weeks later."

He bowed his head. For a moment he was unable to continue. Finally he looked at Julia again. "I'll spare you the details of the condition in which Nancy was found," he said. "It was horrible. She'd been sacrificed."

"Sacrificed?" she gasped.

"There was evidence of drugs in her system. A ceremonial knife was found near the body."

"I began tracing the cult, but I didn't have much success at first. Little by little I gleaned information here and there and pieced it all together. Ultimately I came up with the name Cagliostro. I then heard about Belham. That is why I came here. It is not revenge I'm seeking. What happened to Nancy I'm afraid she brought about herself. I'm sure they have had other victims whom they sacrificed. I want to make sure there are no more in the future. I intend destroying Cagliostro and the entire village of Satanists which he controls."

"Belham...Satanists? Oh, no," Julia said. "You must be mistaken. There are no such practices going on here."

"How can you say that? You've only recently arrived in Belham. I have been here for a good many weeks and I have had a chance to investigate. The house in which you live is where their rites are held. I have no proof, but I am sure sacrifices have been performed there."

Julia suddenly felt horror-struck. She remembered the dream in which she had carried the child and given it to Adrian, who put it on the altar in the secret room. But it had been only a dream, she reminded herself, remembering too that no one had reported a child missing.

"Surely you are mistaken, Dr. Dunston," Julia argued.

"I am not mistaken. Your father is the Devil's advocate, if not the Devil himself. There is too much evidence in that direction for me to be mistaken. He knows that I am suspicious of his carryings-on. That is why he sent you to put a spell on Danny. It was supposed to be a warning."

"Who is Danny?"

"My younger brother. I shouldn't have brought him here, but when my parents died I had no other choice. It was you who came to my cottage last night to put Danny under that spell. You have got to get him out of it."

Julia looked startled and confused. "But I know nothing of trances or spells or any such thing. I dreamed I was at your house. But it was only a dream. My father said I'd seen you and your brother at the inn, and it stuck in my mind and recurred last night in a dream."

"I've never been to the inn and neither has my brother. I had never seen you before last night when I saw you standing in front of Danny, pressing his temples and making strange signs on his head."

"But it wasn't me. I only dreamed I was there."

"Talk sense, girl. How could it have been a dream if I saw you with my very own eyes? I spoke to you. You ran out into the rain. I would have followed you if it hadn't been for the strange spell you put on Danny."

"But I don't remember being there, except in my dream. Besides, I couldn't have been there. My father locked me in my room because I had been guilty of sleepwalking of late."

"Your father locked you in your room?"

"Yes. I've been having very strange dreams. Just the other night I dreamed—" She interrupted herself. She didn't think she should tell him about having dreamed of kidnapping a small girl from her bed.

"Yes," he urged. "What did you dream?"

"Nothing," she said, putting him off. "It was just a silly dream. It meant nothing."

He gave her a suspicious look. After a moment he said, "I believe your father is trying to put you under his control, if he hasn't already done so. You must get out of that house before it is too late. I have a feeling that you are not completely in his power yet, but your fear of that stained-glass window makes me suspect that it won't be long before you will take your place beside Cagliostro."

"What does the stained-glass window have to do with anything? I saw no window behind the altar."

"You did, but you refused to recognize it." He paused to put emphasis on his next remark. "The window is in the shape of a giant crucifix."

Her eyes widened. She had heard stories of how devils and vampires cower before the Christian symbol. "You don't mean...." Her voice faltered.

"I believe your father is bent upon your becoming an advocate of Satan's. He will consecrate you into the hierarchy of his cult. You are a Cagliostro, he claims. That holds much prestige and many privileges in Satanic worship."

"No, you're wrong. My father...the Cagliostros are not involved in that sort of thing anymore," she argued.

"How do you know? Are you even certain the man who says he is your father actually is your father? You might not be a Cagliostro after all. How can you be so positive that you're his daughter?"

"He says my birth certificate is among his papers."

"But he never showed it to you?"

Julia shook her head.

"Then it is quite possible that you are not his daughter. You said your records at the orphanage showed that you were the child of a Bridget Bishop. Your father may not be the man he claims he is."

"That can't be. My Aunt Rose said—"

He cut her off. "But how do you know she is your Aunt Rose? Remember, the whole town is controlled by Cagliostro. They will do and say whatever he tells them to do and say. Who is this Aunt Rose you mention?"

"The woman who owns the inn." She told him quickly of her arrival in Weaver and then in Belham. She told of her little trick to get lodging at the inn. "They didn't want me there at all. They told me to get out of Belham."

"They thought you were a spy like myself, most likely, an

enemy of their cause."

"If they didn't want me in Belham, why did they suddenly change their minds when I told them my name was Julia Carson and that my mother was Bridget Bishop?"

Dunston scratched his chin. "Bridget Bishop was obviously someone of importance in the town. Possibly she was closely akin to Cagliostro."

"She was his wife. And she was my mother."

"No, I don't think that's true. I don't believe any man as cruel or as evil as Dr. Cagliostro would ever take a wife. He is too debauched for that."

Julia bristled. "He is my father and I love him very much."

"Julia," he said softly. "Please listen to me. The man who calls himself your father is evil. He means evil for you as well. Run away from him. Get out of that house before he possesses you completely. He can do that, believe me. Once you are consecrated to Satan you can never be free of him. Cagliostro means to destroy you, Julia. Oh, perhaps he will not do it physically, but there are other more terrible ways to destroy. Run away. Run away from him before it is too late. Please, Julia, listen to what I tell you."

"Run away? And where would you suggest I run, Dr. Dunston. To you, perhaps?"

She did not want to listen to anything more this man had to say. She wanted to have time to reason things out for herself. She had to get away from Dunston. She had to be alone to think.

"Go anywhere you wish. Only make sure it is outside of Belham and away from the man who claims to be your father."

"No!" she said sharply. "My father is a good and kind man. He is not what you say. I love him very much. Don't say those horrible things about him. They aren't true, I tell you!" She turned and ran out of the room.

By the time Dunston reached the door, she was gone.

CHAPTER TWENTY

Her mind was completely muddled. How dare he say such things about her father, the man who'd taken her in and given her a whole new, wonderful life? Of course he was her father. The entire town knew of Bridget Bishop and they all knew that Bridget Bishop was married to Dr. Lucius Cagliostro, or the man who now calls himself by that name.

A thought popped into her mind: what about the secret room? And she remembered giving the child to Adrian. Could there possibly be a some element of truth in what Dunston said?

No. The whole thing was utter nonsense. Dunston was grieving over the loss of his wife. The man was too young to bear up under that grief. He was mad. He was dangerous. She would have to warn her father.

"Julia," Matilda said when the girl burst into the house. "What is it?"

"Where's Father? I must see him."

She burst into his study. He'd been writing in a large ledger and looked up sharply when she dashed in.

"What is it, Julia?" He helped her to a chair and knelt beside it.

"Oh, Father, it isn't true what he said. Tell me it isn't true," she sobbed.

"Julia, try to compose yourself. What isn't true? Who said what?" He patted her hand and tried to calm her.

"Dr. Dunston," she blurted. "He said you weren't my father," she said. "You are my father, aren't you? Tell me you are."

"Of course I'm your father. I told you before. Do you need proof?"

He walked to his desk and unlocked a drawer, taking out a steel box. He rummaged inside and extracted a formal-looking document. Coming back to Julia he handed her the paper. "Here. This is your birth certificate. See for yourself."

She took the paper, her eyes scanning it quickly. She saw the names Bridget Bishop and Lucius Bishop. She was born on the thirteenth day of August at one minute after midnight in the town of Belham, Massachusetts. The document gave her weight at birth, the time of birth, and that her father and mother had decided the child would be named Bridget. She looked up through her tears and smiled.

"Oh, Father, I'm so ungrateful. How could I have doubted you?"

"There, there, Julia. Think nothing of it. I should have shown you the certificate the day you arrived. It just escaped my mind, like so many other things of late." He paused. "Now, do you want to see the official document that changed my name from Bishop to Cagliostro?"

"Oh, no. I believe anything you say, Father. I could never doubt you again."

"Good." He went toward the door she had left ajar and closed it softly. He came back and sat in a chair beside her. "Now, tell me about this meeting with Dr. Dunston. Just exactly what did he say? But why did you meet him, child?"

"I was concerned about the dreams I had, especially the one in which I saw him. Then, when he made those accusations about my having put a spell on his brother, I had to find out what it all meant."

She shuddered. "He isn't well, Father. The things he believes are quite frightening."

"What things?"

"Well, first he believes that the all the people of the town of Belham are Satanists. Second, that you are the Devil's advocate, if not the Devil himself."

"I see," her father said. "What else did the good Dr. Dunston say?"

"Oh, Father, we must be tolerant of him. His wife died some kind of horrible death that obviously affected his mind. I don't really believe the man knows what he is saying."

"His wife?"

"Yes. He told me his wife's name was Nancy, and that she'd gotten mixed up with some religious cult that delved into Devil worship. She was found dead under very terrible circumstances."

"Nancy Dunston." He looked vague.

"Did you know her, Father?"

He shook his head. "No, no. Go on, please."

She told him of Dunston's background, his involvement with medicine, psychiatry, and, finally, of the strange religion that glorified Satan which he stumbled upon. "He said he did some research on Devil worship and ran across the name Cagliostro. Someone he met told him there was a Cagliostro living in Belham. He must have associated your name with a similar name connected with the cult his wife was involved with. He's come here for some terrible reason, Father. You must be careful of him. He thinks you're someone else. He means to do you harm, I'm sure of it."

Her father smiled suddenly. "Have no fears, my dear. We are very capable of handling any kind of trouble that crops up here in Belham. You forget that Adrian is always on hand when needed. I'll speak with him. He will know what to do."

"Adrian?" Julia said, suddenly brightening. "He's returned?"

"If he hasn't, I'll be able to reach him. Between the three of us, we will handle Dr. Dunston and his quarrelsome meddling. Now, young lady, I believe you had best rest yourself for an hour or so. You look worn out. The man upset you, I see."

"I must admit he did," Julia said as she got up out of her chair. "I suppose it was because I let myself feel sorry for him at first. He seemed so scared and young and so worried and lost. But then, when he began his ravings, I knew I had to be rid of him." She looked anxiously toward her father. "You do believe I did the right thing in telling you all this?"

"Of course you did the right thing, child. Remember. You must always come to me when you're worried or upset or frightened. I'll always be with you, and I will always help you, so never hesitate."

Julia walked with him out of the study. They started up the staircase. "I do wish these dreams would end," she told him. "They are upsetting me more than I care to admit. It was the dream, after all, that brought Dr. Dunston here in the first place. I don't understand how he could have seen me with his brother, or how I could have seen him. I'm certain I was in that cottage last night, and he swears that I was there."

"More of his insanity. It's possible the man is adept at manipulating people's subconscious. You said yourself he'd been educated in psychiatry and matters dealing with the mind. There are such things as thought transference, hypnosis, and the powers of suggestion. He might have used any of these mental devices on you when he saw you at the inn."

Julia looked at him sideways. She was tempted to tell him Dunston's claim that he had never been to the inn and never saw her before last night in his cottage. But Aunt Rose had agreed with her father that Dunston and his brother *had* been at the inn the night she arrived.

"I wouldn't think anymore about it, Julia. Rest yourself and put it all out of your mind. In the meantime, I will endeavor to reach our friend Adrian and ask him to help us cope with this Dunston fellow."

At the door to her room her father pecked her forehead and again told her to rest.

"Father," she said, biting down on her lower lip. "I had the strangest experience when I entered that church to meet Dr. Dunston. The place was stripped bare, but I had the terrible sensation of fear. I couldn't understand why." She gave him a bewildered look. "I still can't figure out why I felt so afraid."

"I believe you walked all the way into Belham, did you not? All that fresh air and exercise, and then going inside a dank, dusty old place that had been shut up for years and years. The air in there is stale and thin. I don't believe it was fear that made you shiver, Julia, as much as it was a lightness of the head due to a lack of oxygen. The heat of the day, your long walk in the sun, all had a lot to do with it. It wasn't fear that upset your system, it was something in your body's chemistry that acted up. I wouldn't worry about it."

"Dr. Dunston said that I was being possessed and that it was the stained-glass window that made me cower with fear."

To her surprise her father laughed loudly. "A stained-glass window? Well, well. What won't the man come up with? I'm the advocate of Satan and you are afraid of stained-glass windows. The man deserves whatever happens to him."

He turned and went down the corridor.

CHAPTER TWENTY-ONE

Sleep came quickly, without warning.

One minute she was awake, the next she was in a deep sleep. She could feel the warmth of the afternoon sun on her face as it poured through the window, cutting a path across the bed. A worry line inched across her brow. People kept saying terrible things to her. The gypsy, the medium, and now Dunston. Daughter of evil. Satan worshippers. Trouble.

She shifted uneasily in her sleep.

A sudden chill crept over her. She groped for the coverlet and pulled it up around her. The sun left the sky and she found herself in darkness. It was cold and wintry, bleak and damp. She sensed something being pressed into her hand. She tried to open her eyes but they were fastened shut.

"It's time," she heard someone say. She wanted to raise her lids but they were too heavy. Then a wandering current of air seemed to lift her up from the bed and buoy her up into the air. The weightlessness touched her eyes and she opened them. She knew she could see but there was nothing to see. She was awake, she kept telling herself, yet she could not speak or feel. There was only blackness and silence. She held something in her hand but did not know what it was.

"Julia," she heard the voice say. "It's time."

Then the blackness lifted and she found herself walking along a road. It was night and the stars had left the sky. Only the flame-yellow moon gleamed down, lighting her path. The road seemed familiar, yet she did not know where she was or where she was going.

Her sense of touch returned and she felt the object that had been placed in her hand. She raised her arm. The glint of a huge knife blade flashed back at her. She stared at the knife, not knowing where it had come from or why she carried it. The ornate handle fit her palm neatly. It felt comfortable to hold. She tightened her grip without realizing it and liked the smooth warmth of it in her palm.

The road narrowed into a footpath. Ahead she saw the outline of a large cottage with its tapered brick chimney, its thatched roof, its tiny garden so trim and tidy. A light burned in several windows. The place looked cozy and warm and the chill in her bones sent her hurrying toward it.

She pushed open the little wooden gate and walked up the path. The door was closed. Through the window she saw a familiar figure sprawled before the fire. A book lay open in his lap. His pipe smoldered on a table next to him. His eyes were closed, his chin hung slack, his mouth slightly open. His breathing was even and regular. A thick wave of sand-colored hair spilled over his forehead.

Julia unconsciously tightened her grip on the ceremonial knife and eased open the door of the cottage. She stood at the threshold staring down at the sleeping figure of Dr. Dunston. His face looked so handsome, so youthful, so peaceful. His dreams were pleasant dreams, she thought, not like her dreams. Why should he be permitted lovely dreams when hers were so terrifying?

"He is trying to steal away your home, your whole future," a voice told her. "He is a threat to everything you want out of life. He means you harm, Julia. The man does not deserve to live."

Slowly she walked toward the chair, lifting the knife high into the air. She stood poised. The knife suddenly felt too heavy to keep aloft. With a quick move of her arm she brought it down.

Dunston opened his eyes and saw the knife blade aiming for his heart. He rolled out of the chair, throwing himself sideways. The table beside him toppled with him as he hit the floor. A split second later he was back on his feet. He grabbed Julia's arm and wrenched the knife from her grip.

She fought him as a tigress would fight to protect her cubs. She clawed and scratched and hissed and growled. His strength was too great for her, however. She felt her arm going numb. He wrenched the wrist back until she felt it was going to break. Her palm opened and the knife clattered to the floor.

Dunston drew back his hand and slapped her as hard as he could across the face. Julia's head flew back. Her cheek stung. She felt the strange blackness begin to lift. The ache in her cheek was so painful she could think of nothing else. She buried her face in her hands. The darkness got brighter and brighter until she thought it would blind her. Whatever had pressed against her eyes and mouth was no longer there. Her eyes rolled in her head and she fell to the floor.

"Julia, open your eyes." Someone was rubbing her wrists and patting her cheeks. "Julia, Julia."

Her lids fluttered and opened. It took a moment or two before Dunston's face came into focus. The room kept spinning around and she wanted desperately for it to stop. There were a million bees buzzing around inside her brain. There was a stinging on her cheek.

"Are you all right now?" Dunston asked.

"What happened? Where am I?"

"You're in my cottage. You're safe here. Come, let me help you up."

Julia looked around and saw that she was lying on the floor. She didn't know how she'd gotten there. Then her eyes traveled toward the hearth rug. There, lying at the edge of it, was the ceremonial knife which she had held in her hand. She recognized it and remembered seeing its blade in her dreams. Suddenly she remembered seeing Dunston asleep in the chair. She remembered entering the cottage and standing over him, knife raised high.

"Oh, no," she groaned, again burying her face in her hands. "It wasn't me. It wasn't me. It couldn't have been me," she wailed.

She felt him put his arms around her and cradle her to him. "It is over now, Julia. You were in a trance. You didn't know what you were doing."

"I tried to kill you. I was going to stab you," she said in a half-hysterical voice.

"But you didn't. I'm quite alive and well. I awoke just in time."

"But I wanted to murder you."

"The important thing is that you didn't kill me. Listen to me, Julia. Tonight should be proof enough that what I told you is true. Your father put you into that trance and instructed you to come here and kill me. He is responsible for your coming last night to bewitch my brother. Why he did that, I don't know. Perhaps knowing that I'm wise to him, he wants to do everything terrible to me that he can think of." He shook her gently without realizing it. "Surely you believe me now."

Julia shook her head. "I don't know. I just don't know," she moaned.

"You must believe me. Julia, please. Listen to what I tell you. You must not go back to Cagliostro's house. Your father—if that is who he is—is an evil man. You must face that. Surely you know now that it was he who has been causing you to have these nightmares you mentioned. I can readily believe the awful things he's had you do."

"No, please, I don't want to talk about it. I want to go home. I want to get out of here."

"You can't leave here now. You mustn't. Going back to that house will only mean your doom. Julia, for God's sake, listen to reason." He reached over and picked up the knife. "You know you came here carrying this in your hand. You know you stood over me, intent upon burying this blade in my heart. You know that, don't you?" he demanded, shaking her hard. "Don't you?"

"Yes, yes," Julia cried. She knew what he said was true.

"And yet, knowing he sent you here to kill me, you still want to return to him?"

"But he didn't send me."

"Who did then? Did you come of your own accord? Did you want to murder me? If so, why?"

"I don't know. I don't know," Julia sobbed. She shook her head from side to side and tried to get things clear in her mind. Everything remained a blur. She wanted to run and fling herself off a cliff or drown herself in the sea. She wanted to die. Her head throbbed painfully, her stomach was tied in knots, her nerves were worn and frayed beyond repair.

"Julia, try to think sensibly. You must know that your father is behind your coming here tonight. You told him about our meeting, didn't you?"

"Yes, yes, yes!" She collapsed in a fit of crying.

Dunston straightened her up, forcing her to look into his eyes. "And he told you to come here tonight and kill me."

"No. It was a dream. It was only a dream."

"A dream he manufactured," Dunston said.

"I went to my room to rest. It was in the afternoon." She caught herself and stopped. Her eyes moved toward the open door and she saw the darkness of the night outside. "I have been asleep the whole of the day. How could that be?"

"He put you into a trance. For God's sake, Julia, can't you see that. He is bewitching you nightly and sending you out to do his devilish work."

"No. I won't believe that. It isn't true."

"You must believe it. Don't be a fool. Face facts. Look, think back to your other dreams. You told me they were disturbing you, that you were worried about them. You were here last night and you put my brother under some kind of spell, because I saw you. You know now that you came here tonight to murder me. Surely you must realize how dangerous your dreams are. What other dreams have you had?"

Dazed, unable to think straight, Julia said, "I carried a child to the house the other night and gave her to Adrian."

"Adrian? Who's Adrian?"

Julia stared straight ahead of her, as if again in a trance. "He works for my father. He comes and goes. He is very handsome and polite. He told me to give him the child. He took it to the secret room."

"Secret room?" He was uncomfortably aware that her eyes had suddenly gotten lifeless and she spoke in a strange, monotonous voice.

"Anubis guards it. It's in the parlor. Adrian put the child on the altar and told me to go back to bed. I didn't want him to take her but he said it was the best thing for her."

"Oh, good God." He put his head in his hands and tried to hold back the sickening horror he felt.

Julia suddenly shook herself. She came alive again. "But it was just a dream, Dunston. I didn't take any child. Father and I went into Belham the next day, when I told him how upset I was over the dream. He asked everyone. No one was missing any little girl. We even went to the very same cottage I'd seen in my dreams and we asked the parents if their little girl was missing. They told us she wasn't home but that she was safe and with her grandparents."

"And you believed them?"

"Why shouldn't I have believed them?"

"I tried to tell you yesterday, Julia. The whole village is under Cagliostro's control. You will be too if you return to that house. These people are all Satanists. No one is safe from being sacrificed to Lucifer, the king of hell. They'd gladly give up their own children if that is what is asked of them. They think it's an honor to die for the love of Lucifer and his advocates. Your father merely sent you to collect that little girl." Again he shook his head. "It is so ugly and disgusting."

Julia sat staring into space. This wasn't happening. What he said wasn't true. Yet she was fully awake and conscious now. She was in Dunston's house, there was no doubting that. She had carried a knife to this place and intended planting that knife in Dunston's chest. She had been here the night before and had made strange signs on a little boy's head.

"Your brother?" she asked, slightly dazed.

"He's in there," Dunston told her, nodding toward a closed door.

"Is he...?"

"No, he isn't dead, if that is what you were going to ask. He is in some kind of catatonic state. I can't arouse him. He just sits and stares and says nothing. I don't know what it all means. Why Danny? What does Cagliostro want with my brother?"

Julia found herself saying, "Adrian wants him."

Dunston jerked his head up and stared at her. "Adrian wants him? What do you mean?"

Julia rubbed her hand across her eyes. "What did I say?"

"You said Adrian wanted Danny."

"Oh, did I?" The room was beginning to spin around again. "I wonder why I said that."

Dunston studyied her intently. The pupils of her eyes were dilated. He felt her pulse. It was almost nonexistent. Quickly he got to his feet and poured a jigger of brandy into a glass. He brought it back and forced her to sip it. Julia choked on the first swallow. She felt the burning liquid sear her throat and creep into her stomach, warming it.

"Who is this Adrian? Do you know anything about him other than that he works for your father?"

Julia took a deep breath and found the room settling down again. "He came to me the night I arrived in Belham. I saw him again in the secret room. He's a very nice man, very soft-spoken and polite. He was exceedingly attentive to me."

Dunston gave her an annoyed look. "I'll bet." He grabbed her again and shook her gently. "Don't you know that Adrian is the name by which Lucifer is sometimes known?"

Julia blanched. "Lucifer?"

"Yes, Lucifer. The fallen angel. The ruler of hell. The Devil himself."

She stared at him in disbelief.

"Julia, you must listen to me when I say you are living in a den of vipers. You cannot go back to that house. I won't let you. If I have to lock you here in this cottage, I will do it before I will permit you to leave and return to Cagliostro. Please say you'll stay. Let me prove to you that what I say is all true. I'll guarantee that your terrible dreams will disappear. I realize that you are reluctant to give up the father you spent your life trying to find. But you must not think of him as a father but as a demon, a devil, an evil sorcerer. He only means to make you a part of his evil ways. Stay here, Julia. Let me protect you. Let me help you."

"But I love him very much," she sobbed.

Dunston put his arms around her. "You can't afford that kind of love, Julia. It will destroy you. I'm sorry. You know, don't you, that the man represents evil? If you are indeed his daughter, then you must deny him at all costs."

Evil. Daughter.

"Daughter of evil," Julia said absentmindedly. She knew that what Dunston was saying might very well be true. Yet she didn't want to believe him. She wanted to go home. "Daughter of evil," she said again.

Dunston looked down at her. His face was grim and creased with worry.

From out of nowhere Julia suddenly heard the strange chanting and remembered Adrian leading the people to the secret room. Then something else came clearly to mind. She saw herself standing before Anubis. Matilda stood behind her. She heard Matilda say, "Your time is not yet come. You must not appear until all is ready for you." The chanting continued. It droned on and on, echoing inside her head.

Suddenly she knew Dunston was right. It hit her like a thunderbolt.

She collapsed in a spasm of tears. The home she'd wanted for so long was being taken away from her. She would have to give it up.

There was nothing else for her to do.

CHAPTER TWENTY-TWO

She was back at the very beginning. She'd lost all she had gained. All her efforts had been in vain.

Would she have to return to New York? No, she'd never be able to face Elizabeth, Allyson and, particularly, Margaret. Her pride would never permit that. Daughter of evil, she remembered the medium say. She remembered all of the trouble she'd taken to break into the orphanage just to have it all go up in smoke.

The old gypsy, the séance, the long trek to Rossmore, the exhausting train ride to Peabody, then to Weaver, then to Belham. And for what? Where had it led? What had she gotten for all her trouble? A scant number of happy days and now all was to be swiftly taken away from her.

Dunston had to be right, though. There was evil in the house she'd run away from. There had to be. Her first impression of the place should have warned her. The secret room with its bizarre trappings, the dreary atmosphere that permeated the place.

Her dreams hadn't been dreams at all. Everything she'd seen and experienced had been real. The townspeople *had* come to the secret room to pay homage to the Devil. She *had* taken a child and delivered it into Adrian's hands. She *had* cast a spell on poor little Danny. Most frightening of all was the fact that she knew she had deliberately tried to knife Dunston to death.

She had not acted on her own volition, that she did know. Someone or something had driven her to it. But who? Was it indeed her father? Or was someone else forcing these nightmares on her, using her for their evil purposes? Perhaps Adrian was behind the terrible trances she was placed in. It was he, after all, who had led the group of people to the house—the people who had chanted and reveled behind the protection of Anubis. He was the one who seemed to appear and disappear at will. As attracted as she was to the man, she had to admit that Adrian was a complete mystery. It was he who had waited for her to fetch the little girl. And it was he who had placed the child on the altar.

Her spirits lifted a bit. Her father wasn't responsible for any of it. It was Adrian's doing.

She heard Dunston coming from his brother's room and she jumped up, eager to tell him what she knew.

"It isn't my father at all," she said excitedly as Dunston came into the room. "Adrian is the one behind it. He's the one who makes me act out my dreams."

Dunston looked very serious and shook his head slowly. "You mustn't torture yourself by trying to find excuses for Cagliostro, Julia. If I'm not mistaken, Adrian and Cagliostro are one and the same man."

She stared at him. "What are you saying? How can that be?"

"I don't know. But what I did learn about Satanists is that they are capable of just about anything. Some of them—especially seasoned ones like Cagliostro—can change themselves at will. They never age if they don't want to. They can inhabit whatever body they like." He gave her a stern look. "You read of some of Count Cagliostro's exploits. You know what the man was capable of doing. Over the years those powers have grown stronger and stronger. You're snatching at straws, I'm afraid. It would be better for you to accept the truth and live with it. It will prove easier in the end."

"The end. Where is the end?"

"The ultimate end is in the grave. But there is an interim period wherein one must be as happy as one can be. Being born is easy enough; dying is easier. It is the period in between that is difficult. Try not to make it more difficult by being unhappy."

"I was happy. You took it away from me."

"But that was a false happiness. It would have ended more disastrously for you if you were not alerted to what evils lurked around you. Look at me, Julia. Tell me, would you have preferred that we never met, that I had never warned you about Cagliostro and the Satanists of Belham?"

She moved away from his touch. "I don't know, Dunston. You have taken the brief happiness I had away. I don't know if you were right in doing so."

"What must I do to convince you? Remember your dreams, Julia. Remembering those terrible things should keep you from going back to the evil which surrounded you in that house. You would have been guilty of murder if I hadn't awakened last night." He glanced toward Danny's room. "And God only knows what other evil you're capable of when under the spell of Cagliostro."

"But how do you know my father is responsible? Perhaps he too is under the evil influence of someone."

"Cagliostro will show himself in time and you will have your proof. Until then, stay with me and let me keep you safe. I realize that there will be strong efforts made to reclaim you. Cagliostro is well aware of what went wrong last night. He'll try everything in his power to get you back, but I'm prepared for him. I may not be as knowledgeable about Satanism as he, but I do know how to exorcise evil spirits and to protect myself and others with holy relics and pentacles."

"Pentacles?"

"Star-shaped figures, the boundaries of which evil cannot pass over. I will draw one here in the middle of the floor before I leave for Weaver. All you need do is stand in it and no one can harm you."

Julia watched as Dunston proceeded to move all of the furniture from the center of the room. He took up the rugs, exposing the wooden floor. He brought a heavy piece of chalk and began drawing a large circle. The circle—approximately seven- or eight-feet across—was round and perfect and occupied most of the room. After completing the first circle, he drew another inside its circumference. Julia marveled at the evenness of the lines. Inside the two circles Dunston made a five-pointed star, the top point of which pointed toward the front door of the cottage. He drew connecting lines to each point, creating a polygram with five sides in the exact middle of the five-pointed star.

Julia said nothing during the whole operation. She watched with interest and fascination. Yet when the basic form of the pentacle was completed, she found herself shying away from it.

"Don't be afraid of it," he said. "The pentacle is the only device I know of that wards off evil. Once you stand inside its boundaries, nothing evil can get near you. But if you leave these circles, you will be at Cagliostro's mercy."

Dunston resumed his precise drawing. He drew strange little figures between the outer circles. He placed a different sign at each point of the star. Then, using the point directed toward the door as a base, he began building the picture of a ram's or goat's head. The point toward the door was the chin, the points going off to the right and left were its ears and the two points atop each held one of the ram's horns.

"You're an artist," she said.

"Just something I picked up in my spare time."

He finished the pentacle by fetching candles and placing them at three strategic positions around the outside of the circle. He drew a match from his pocket and lit the candles one by one.

"Keep these burning at all times," he said. "There is a supply of them here in this cupboard. Don't let them go out under any circumstances."

"I'll remember," Julia said, still feeling shy of the strange drawing in the center of the room.

Then Dunston took a resinous substance and sprinkled it just outside the circumference of the outer circle. He blessed each drop with the sign of the cross saying, "Asafoetida."

Then he fetched five silver cups and poured what he told Julia was holy water into them and place one in each of the valleys of the star. He put a horseshoe at each point of the star and before each horseshoe he placed mandrake root. He went into the kitchen and returned with garlands of garlic and several crucifixes.

"Put these around your neck if any danger threatens," he told her.

"Garlic?"

"It's a very powerful charm against evil. Don't scoff at it. Wear it when you find yourself in danger. Promise me."

She nodded but wrinkled her nose at the garlands of garlic.

"Now," Dunston said, putting the finishing touches to the pentacle and glancing around. "I'll bring Danny here and put him inside the pentacle's protection. I must go to Weaver to fetch the housekeeper."

"Housekeeper?"

"It would not be very proper for you and I to go on sharing this cottage without benefit of a chaperone. I've arranged for a woman I learned about to come and stay. Her name is Sarah Carrier. She's from Weaver and there aren't very many people in Weaver who look kindly upon Belhamites."

Julia remembered the dreary little town and the strange character who drove her to Belham.

"The people in Weaver know what goes on here. They try their best to do everything they can to abolish the rites, but they've never been very successful."

Julia thought of her mother and what her Aunt Rose had told her about the people from Weaver. If what Dunston said was true, then Bridget Bishop might well have been taken as a Satanist and set upon by the people from Weaver. They might have carried her away and put her to death. She shuddered at the horrible thought. It was too terrible to think about, but it did explain a lot—if what Dunston said was true.

Again she thought of her father and what he had told her about her mother. He'd said that Bridget Bishop had been ill and was running away from him. Was it possible that her mother was running away to protect her baby from the evil that Cagliostro intended for her? Had her mother been trying to spirit her away to safety only to fall into the hands of people from Weaver who disposed of her, knowing she was a Satanist? Had they dealt with the baby by placing it in an orphanage?

It did make sense when she thought of it all in that light. If her father was as evil as Dunston claimed, then he would, of course, lie to her about her mother's death. But why had Aunt Rose told her the truth—if that was the truth?

"You're thinking too hard. Just keep yourself inside the cottage, especially if anyone comes near. Don't, under any circumstances, let anyone inside the house. If they force their way in, seek the protection of the pentacle. They'll try to lure you out where they can claim you, but don't let them." He patted her cheek. "I know how unhappy you must be, but believe me, Julia, it is for the best. Everything will turn out all right. You'll see."

She said nothing. She was still thinking of her mother's fate at the hands of the people from Weaver. If what she thought was true, then were the people from Weaver any better than the people of Belham? She tried to shrug off the thought. What she was thinking was hideous, yet she couldn't help herself.

"I won't be long," Dunston told her. "Be suspicious of everyone and everything. Remember, no one in Belham is free of Cagliostro's influence. Therefore, trust no one. Now, promise me that you won't do anything foolish like run home to Cagliostro. Promise me."

"I promise," she said, but reluctantly.

"Good." He went into his brother's room and returned a moment later with Danny. "Now, watch over Danny. Don't let him wander around. I wish to heaven there was some way you could undo the spell you put on him."

"I wasn't responsible," she said meekly.

"I know you weren't, Julia. I don't blame you, now that I know what really happened. It wasn't your fault; I just wish there was some way in which I could get Danny to come around to his old self."

"Perhaps I could ask Adrian—"

"No," Dunston said sharply. "You are not to go near Adrian or Cagliostro or your house. You are to stay here. Is that clear?"

She nodded, intimidated by his outburst.

He turned to leave but paused at the door. "Remember. Stay inside and don't let anyone in except me."

When he had gone, she stood looking at the closed door, then glanced down at the strange diagram drawn on the floor. She didn't understand it and she felt afraid of it. Slowly her eyes moved to Danny, who sat watching her. He was mute and staring straight into her eyes. She went over to him and put her hand on his hair. It felt soft and silky to the touch. She smoothed it back, tilting his chin up.

"Oh, Danny. I wish I could undo whatever I did. Please don't be angry with me. I didn't know what I was doing at the time. If only I could remember what kind of patterns I traced on your head, I might be able to untrace them. I must have said some kind of words over you, but I don't recall what they were." She could remember nothing at all except coming in out of the rain and staring deep into Danny's eyes.

She'd stared at him. That was it. She'd put him into a hypnotic state. Perhaps she could accomplish it again and wake him out of it. She quickly knelt in front of him, feeling her anxiety and her excitement growing. She looked deep into the boy's eyes, returning his stare.

"That's it, Danny. Look deep into my eyes. That's the way." She tilted his head up and fixed her eyes firmly on his. "You must wake up, Danny," she said. "You are asleep now, but you must wake up. The night is over and it is time to wake up. When I count to three I will snap my fingers and you will awaken."

"One. Two. Three." She snapped her fingers in front of his face. Danny continued to stare at her. Again she counted and snapped her fingers. Nothing happened. Again, a little louder, she counted to three. Again she snapped her fingers. She clapped her hands alongside his ear. Still, Danny remained in his trance.

Feeling beaten, Julia got slowly to her feet. She rumpled the boy's hair and turned dejectedly away. "I tried, Danny. I really tried. I'm sorry," she said as the tears began streaming down her cheeks.

Suddenly she stiffened. Someone outside was calling her name.

CHAPTER TWENTY-THREE

"We're almost there now, Mrs. Carrier," Dunston said as he steered the car down the lane leading to his cottage.

Sarah Carrier huffed. "I don't know why I let you talk me into taking this job. These people here in Belham should all be put to the stake. The state should come in and burn every last one of these heathens."

"Now, Mrs. Carrier, don't worry about the people of Belham. You'll have little or nothing at all to do with them. All I want you to do is keep up the house and watch over my brother and Miss Julia."

"Cagliostro's daughter, huh?"

Dunston shot her a look. "How did you know that?"

Sarah Carrier shrugged her bony shoulders. "I heard. We in Weaver hear everything that goes on in Belham. She stopped there looking for a ride over here. The Belhamites don't do much that we ain't aware of. Of course, we have to be careful what we do too. They have spies in Weaver, you know."

"What do you mean?"

"Those Devil worshipers are always trying to get one of us into their hellish rituals. We found a couple in Weaver who used to sneak over here regularly. We fixed their wagons all right, let me tell you," she said with a hellish chuckle.

Dunston had a good idea of what she meant by "fixing their wagons" and he didn't like to think on it. The people from Weaver, he had learned, were just as sinister as the Satanists, but the difference was that the Weaverites did it in the name of

God, whereas the Belhamites did it in the name of Satan, but there wasn't all that much difference between the people of the two towns. It was just that their evils were done in different names and under different guises.

"This is it," Dunston said as he pulled the car into the drive beside his cottage. "It shouldn't be hard to keep up. It's large, of course, but it's laid out in such a way that it's easy to keep clean."

"Hard work don't bother me none. But I still don't know if I'm doing right by coming over here," Sarah Carrier complained. "If the money weren't so good I'd tell you to go to the Devil." She laughed then. "Now, I guess I shouldn't have said that, should I?"

The minute Dunston opened the door he knew something was wrong. Julia and Danny were huddled in the center of the pentacle.

Mrs. Carrier stood with her mouth opened as she looked at the huddled figures and the drawing on the floor. "What in blazes is this all about?" she asked.

Julia jumped up and rushed at him. "Oh, Dunston, they tried to get us. They came, Aunt Rose and two of the Hastings brothers. Aunt Rose called to me and said she needed to talk to me. I almost went outside until I realized that Aunt Rose could not have known where I was unless she had been told by someone who knew I came here last night. What you say must be true. I didn't go out, Dunston. I got Danny safely into the pentacle and we stayed here until you came."

"Good girl, Julia. You did fine, just fine. And I see Danny's all right, too."

"Yes," Julia said hurriedly, excitedly. She told him about trying to bring Danny out of his spell and how she'd failed.

"Well, at least you tried, Julia. I do appreciate that."

Sarah Carrier bustled forward. "Here. What's all this nonsense? How do you expect me to get the floor clean with all that drawing on it?"

Dunston remembered that Mrs. Carrier was a stranger to the

house. "Oh, Mrs. Carrier. This is Julia and that's my brother Danny." Dunston glanced down at the pentacle. "Don't bother about the floor in this room. Under no circumstances are you to wash away this pentacle."

"Pentacle? What's that?"

"I'll explain it all later. Right now, how about getting yourself settled in. You'll find a room at the back of the kitchen where you can stay. I think we could all use a bit of food right now, so I'd appreciate your getting settled and then starting in to fix us something to eat."

"Let me help," Julia said.

Julia and Sarah Carrier went toward the kitchen. Dunston took Danny by the hand and led him out of the pentacle. "Come along, Dan. I think the immediate danger is over. You might just as well get comfortable in your own room. I'll call you when it's time to eat."

But when it was time to eat, Danny was gone.

"Gone? Where could he have gone?" Julia asked. The boy's room was empty.

"What I can't figure out is how he got out."

"Did you check the windows?" Mrs. Carrier asked. "All the boys I know are always climbing in and out of windows."

The window was open. Dunston looked out. Across the open field he saw the figure of his brother walking slowly toward the woods. "Danny!" he called. A split second later he had dashed out of the room, out of the house, and was running as fast as he could across the field.

Julia and Mrs. Carrier watched as Danny disappeared into the woods with Dunston close on his trail.

"Boys will be boys," Mrs. Carrier said. She sighed. "Well, I'd best get the food back into the warming oven before everything gets cold. No telling when those two will get back here."

The light was beginning to fade by the time Dunston returned with Danny in tow. One look at the boy told Julia that something was wrong. Danny's face was white as a sheet. His eyes were glazed. She laid a hand on his forehead.

"I know, I know," Dunston said quickly when he saw Julia's perplexed expression. "The boy looks feverish but he doesn't feel the least bit hot. You'd better get my medical bag. It's in the closet in my room. I'll get him into bed right away."

Just as night settled around the cottage, Danny started sweating profusely and his whole body began to shake violently. Dunston looked at him with alarm. He shook his head.

"I don't know what it is," he said. "It's nothing I've run across. He has no temperature, no fever, yet he's sweating like a man with malaria. I don't know what's causing the trembling. He'll come apart if I can't get him to stop." He ran his hands through his hair. "If I'd spent more time keeping up with my medical books instead of chasing devils I might be able to diagnose the problem."

"You mustn't start blaming yourself, Dunston," Julia said. "Perhaps it is part of the spell."

Dunston straightened. "Of course. That must be it."

At that moment, Danny began moaning and then he started to gag and choke. Dunston rushed over to him. "He can't breathe," Dunston gasped. He watched as Danny writhed and twisted on the bed, trying desperately to get air into his lungs. His face started to puff up and turn purple. Suddenly Danny got very stiff and then he slumped and went limp. He slipped into unconsciousness.

"Quick, hand me my surgical kit," Dunston ordered. He pulled out a scalpel. Julia averted her eyes as Dunston made an incision in Danny's windpipe and fitted it with a small rubber tube. "I'll have to get him over to the hospital in Peabody," he said as he started wrapping Danny up in the bedclothes. "You stay here with Mrs. Carrier." Dunston looked around. "Where is Mrs. Carrier?"

"She said she was tired and went off to bed."

Dunston picked up his brother and started out of the room. "Remember what I said earlier about not leaving the cottage. Put the bolt on the door and don't let anyone in and don't, regardless of anything, leave this house. I'll be back as soon as I can."

Julia sat listening to the sound of Dunston's car faded into the night. She felt pangs of hunger and remembered that they had not eaten any of the food that had been prepared. She went into the kitchen and saw that Mrs. Carrier's door was closed. Julia fixed herself a tray and carried it into the bedroom. She picked up a book and clicked on the little radio that sat on the nightstand. The music flowed out soft and lovely as she settled herself on the bed and started to eat and read.

She finished the plate of food and was engrossed in the story she was reading when she heard the voices. She glanced at the clock on the bureau and saw that she'd been reading much longer than she'd thought. It was just a few minutes after midnight. Duston had been gone hours. It was not Dunston's voice she heard outside the cottage, however.

A cold, prickly sweat broke out on her skin. They were calling her name. They weren't the same voices she'd heard earlier. Then a man's voice called: "Julia." It sounded like Adrian's voice.

She reminded herself that it was Adrian who was responsible for her terrible dreams. She wouldn't go out to him, although something inside her tempted her to do so. No, she would keep her promise to Dunston. Adrian was behind the terrible things she'd been doing. Adrian had put her up to taking the child with the yellow hair ribbons. Adrian had officiated at the rites after leading the people from Belham into the secret room. It was Adrian with his smooth voice and his handsome face and his polished manners. Adrian was the Devil's advocate.

"Julia. Julia. It's me. Let me in."

"Go away. Leave me alone!" she yelled.

Someone banged on the door. "Let us in, Julia. We only want to talk to you. Your father is worried about you. Please, Julia. Let us talk with you, only for a moment."

"No. Go away. I know what you are now. You'll only make me dream those awful dreams again and you'll make me do those ugly deeds."

"Julia. Listen to me. You must remember that you are Cagliostro's flesh and blood. You don't belong anywhere but in his house—your house. It is your inheritance. You cannot forsake your own father."

"It is not my father I wish to forsake. It's you, Adrian. You are the one who I have run from."

"But why, Julia? What have I done to frighten you away?"

"It isn't what you have done so much as what you are. Dunston told me everything."

"Dunston is your enemy, Julia. Not I. Can't you see that? He has already robbed you of whatever happiness you had found. Is it misery you wish to live in for the rest of your life? Aren't you tired of misery and unhappiness? Haven't you had your fill of it yet? All your life you have yearned for the life you found with your father. How can you turn your back on it so quickly? Why have you allowed Dunston to sway you against your own family so easily?"

"It is my only hope," Julia argued.

There was a long silence.

"In that event," Adrian said, "I will withdraw. I will leave Belham forever and never set foot in the place again if it will please you. My only wish is for you to return to your father, to your rightful place in the world. I want you to be happy, Julia, and if my leaving will bring about that happiness, then I will not hesitate to remove myself from Belham, and your life."

Another long pause followed. Julia thought whoever was outside had gone. She went to the window. Just as she pulled back the curtain to look out, a hideous face of bright orange with flaming red hair and yellow gleaming eyes peered back in at her. She screamed and ran as fast as she could for the protection of the pentacle.

She threw a garland of garlic around her neck and held the crucifix before her as she went. But when she reached the living room, she stared in horror at the floor. There, kneeling, brush and pail in hand, Mrs. Carrier was scrubbing away the pentacle.

"Stop! What are you doing?" Julia shrieked.

It was as if she had not spoken at all. Sarah Carrier continued to scrub away the chalk lines. One by one the points of the star disappeared and with it the picture of the goat's or ram's head. The candles, Julia saw, had been extinguished and the silver cups were overturned, their contents used to wash away the pentacle. The horseshoes were scattered, the mandrake root was put out of sight.

"No, you mustn't do that," Julia yelled. She tried to snatch the brush from Sarah Carrier's hand. In her haste she overturned the pail and the soapy water removed what had remained of the pentacle.

Sarah Carrier stood and went to the door, throwing back the bolt. Julia stood horrified as the door creaked open. Then she saw him. He was dressed all in black. His face was painted a brilliant orange color. His hair, she noticed, was dyed bright red and he had colored his eyes with a yellowish pigment. But the face was his, the body was his, and when he spoke to her, the voice was only too familiar.

"Julia," her father said as he reached out to her.

Julia screamed and threw her hands over her face.

The crucifix that she had been holding clattered to the floor. Sarah Carrier kicked it quickly into a corner as Dr. Cagliostro entered the room. He walked up to Julia and took hold of her hand, lowering it from in front of her eyes.

"Come, my daughter," he said softly. "We must be about our business. The time is getting short."

Julia cringed from him. She backed up against the wall and stood there, her eyes wide with fear. Then, something strange took possession of her and she found herself staring deep into his eyes. She felt her body go numb and limp. Her arms fell weakly to her sides. Her eyes were fixed firmly on her father's hideous face, yet she did not flinch or cringe or back away from him.

She let herself be taken by the hand and led out of the cottage... out into the darkness of the night...out into the road that would take her home.

CHAPTER TWENTY-FOUR

Dunston saw the door standing wide open. He dashed out of the car and into the house. "Julia. Julia," he called. He heard his own voice echoing through the empty rooms. Then he looked down and saw a discarded garland of garlic lying on a recently scrubbed floor. The pentacle was gone, the silver cups overturned, the candles extinguished. The horseshoes were scattered and the mandrake root had vanished.

"Julia! Mrs. Carrier!"

No one answered. Dunston rushed from room to room. He knew they would be empty when he saw that the pentacle was gone. It did not take him very long to figure out who had been responsible for washing it away. He knew Julia would never have done such a thing, and he cursed himself for having put any trust in Sarah Carrier, a woman he scarcely knew. He remembered her speaking of the Satanists' spies in Weaver, and she was, obviously, one of them.

There was only one alternative. He had to find Julia before it was too late, if it wasn't too late already. There was only one place to look for her and he had no time to lose.

The silence on the road warned him against using his car to get to Cagliostro's house. His only chance would be on foot and with the benefit of the element of surprise. They would, of course, be looking out for him, so he told himself he had to be particularly careful.

He went along the road at a steady pace. He was totally lost in his worries about Danny, his fears for Julia, and his determination, and didn't see the woman dressed in black standing just at the edge of the woods. When she spoke his name, he jumped and felt every nerve in his body tingle.

"You can't save her now."

Dunston screwed up his courage and stepped closer to the figure. "Who are you? What do you want?" he demanded. He fingered a small rosary which he had in his pocket. Taking out the beads, he slipped them around his neck. He felt suddenly braver. The tiny silver cross glinted in the light of the yellow moon. He saw the figure raise the long flowing sleeves of her cloak and cover her eyes.

"You cannot save her. It is too late," the figure repeated.

"I know you," Dunston said. "You're the housekeeper."

Matilda nodded. "I mean you no harm. Put the cross to your back so that we can talk."

Dunston hesitated. He fingered the cross for a moment. It was a trick, obviously. "I'm sorry. I cannot do that," he said firmly. "You know it is my only protection. What is it you have to say to me?"

"Put away the cross."

"No. Tell me what you want or I will be on my way."

Matilda kept her eyes turned away from him. "Julia is where she belongs. You must not interfere with her destiny."

"Destiny. You dare speak of destiny?" He thought of his young and innocent wife who'd died at the hands of such people as this. "You didn't consider Nancy's destiny when you brutally sacrificed her to your friend."

"But that was her destiny," Matilda said.

"So I was right. You did kill her. Fiends. You're all fiends," he cried. "Sarah Carrier said you deserved to be burned. I'm in full agreement with her!"

Matilda remained undaunted and unafraid of him. "Sarah Carrier *was* burned at the stake many, many years ago. The Sarah Carrier you spoke with was only an image of the Sarah Carrier we counted among our fold."

"What are you saying?"

"I am saying that the Sarah Carrier you saw was no woman at all, but merely a vision which Cagliostro sent to help him with his plan."

"His plan to reclaim Julia," Dunston finished.

"Julia belongs to him. She can know no other life but that for which she was intended. Bridget Bishop was wrong in thinking she could protect her child from Cagliostro."

"Bridget Bishop? What do you know of Julia's mother?"

"Only that she discovered that Cagliostro and her sister, Rose, were deeply in love with one another. And Cagliostro wanted the child sacrificed to the Master. Bridget took the child and ran out into the night. Unfortunately, the people from Weaver caught her and snuffed out her life. They were not as harsh in their treatment of the child, however. They thought disposing of it in an orphanage would be punishment enough. They never thought that child would someday return to fulfill her true destiny."

"To be sacrificed? Where is Julia now?"

"Where else but where she belongs. I was sent to warn you."

"About what?"

"If you want your brother Danny to recover, you will not lift a finger to help Julia. You must choose which is more important to you: Julia or your little brother. Remember, Julia is a girl you scarcely know; Danny is your only family."

"Just because I scarcely know the girl, I can't turn my back on her and let her fall victim to whatever you people have in store for her. I have no other alternative but to do what I can to save the girl from your terrible decrees."

"Then your brother will die," Matilda said evenly. She raised her arm and pointed a bony finger. "You have been warned. Go away from here. Do not proceed any farther. Go to your brother in Peabody and you will find him fully recovered by the time you arrive there. Take him and never return to Belham again. Forget Julia. It is too late for her anyway."

"No," Dunston swore.

"The girl is happy where she is. She wants only to be with

Him. Why do you persist on interfering where you are not welcome?"

"I am trying to save a girl's life in spite of herself. It is too late for the rest of you, or I would do everything I could to save you also. Julia hasn't been consecrated as yet—this I'm certain of."

Matilda nodded her head. "True, she has not been consecrated. However, that is but a matter of time. Now that she is back where she belongs, she will be consecrated two days hence. At the stroke of midnight on the thirteenth day of August, the twenty-first anniversary of her birth, Julia will be given to the Master. You can do nothing to prevent that from happening. It has been decreed. The Great One had told us that she would return in time for this sacred rite."

Her eyes sparkled and glinted. "Our Master has told us time and time again that a young and beautiful virgin would come to us and save us from the misfortunes that were destined to befall us through the instigation of a nonbeliever who takes up residence in Belham. We knew who you were the day you and your brother arrived here. He told us. Adrian, Lucifer, call him what you wish. He tells us all."

She leveled her blazing eyes on Dunston. "We allowed you to take up residence here, knowing that once you'd ensconced yourself in Belham, the young maid would soon follow, and the prophecy would be fulfilled. Without Julia it was prophesied that you would sow only trouble and misery for all the members of our family. But Julia *has* shown up, and she is our protection from whatever trouble you meant to cause us. We will do everything to keep you from her."

"I intend finding her and bringing her back under my protection."

"Then you will lose your little brother. He will be dead the minute you take Julia away."

Dunston felt driven back. He tried to think of what should be done. He knew now that the threats Matilda was making were not idle ones. They would do what they threatened to do. He would lose Danny if he interfered with Julia's consecration to Satan.

What could he do? He had to think of something. Julia's consecration wasn't to take place for two more days. He would have to construct a well-devised plan. He wouldn't be able to rush blindly into Cagliostro's house and spirit her away before their very eyes. In so doing, Danny would die. There had to be a way of saving both of them. There had to be a way.

He glared at Matilda. She knew she held the upper hand. She turned, tossing her head high in defiance, and disappeared into the darkness of the night. Dunston stood there until she was out of sight. Then he turned and strolled slowly back toward his cottage. He racked his brain, trying to come up with a solution to his dilemma. Nothing came to him. It was Danny or Julia. He would have to make a choice.

As he walked he continued to finger the cross of the rosary beads he was wearing around his neck. Something made him look down at the tiny crucifix. His eyes were drawn to it, like a pin to a magnet.

"Of course," Dunston said. "If I protect Danny with every holy relic I can get my hands on, no one can touch him. No curse can be put on him. It will bounce off the relics and fly back like a boomerang to the person who cast it." He chastised himself for not having thought of that simple solution before this.

But he would have to work quickly, he told himself. He would drive to Peabody again and arrange for Danny's protection. He would surround the boy with chalices of holy water. Every holy relic he could find would take a place on or about Danny's bed. He would surround the boy with every conceivable charm and talisman. He would immerse him in a tub of holy water if necessary. He'd make a pentacle under his bed. He'd isolate him in a sea of holy protection. Nothing would penetrate the wall of defense Dunston vowed to build. And then he would come back and attend to Julia's safety.

He quickened his steps and once inside his cottage, he stripped it of everything he thought he would need. He found garlands of garlic, the horseshoes, the chalk, the mandrake root. He realized he would have to stop at a church and collect more holy water. They would possibly have some at the hospital, but he could not take the chance of their being out of it. He would need more candles. They would need the blessing of a priest. He had enough of the resinous substance to sprinkle on the outside of the circles.

He calculated what he needed to get and how long it would take to procure. He figured the length of time he needed to reach Peabody and return. He glanced at his watch. He would have to hurry. He could not take the chance of waiting until the very last minute to snatch Julia out of their clutches.

He piled his collection into the trunk of the car and filled the backseat with books, clothing, and several pieces of furniture. He decided to stop at the inn and let them think he'd accepted the ultimatum and had chosen to save his brother's life.

Julia's Aunt Rose was sitting on a chair before the front door when he drove up. The door to the inn was wide open. Inside, Dunston saw the Hastings boys bent over a game of cards. The night had turned suddenly warm, although a breeze was moving the leaves of the trees, causing a rustling sound that sounded not unlike a death rattle.

Rose stood when Dunston braked his car. He got out and walked over to her.

"I thought I'd drop off the keys to my house," he said. "I couldn't find old Mr. Hastings at his house."

"He's inside at a card game. I'll give him the keys." She looked him in the eyes. "Are you leaving us, Dr. Dunston?"

"You know perfectly well I'm leaving," he said, not bothering to hide his anger or irritation.

Rose laughed. "Well, I can't say I blame you for making the choice you made."

Dunston frowned. "Do you people know everything that happens the minute it happens?"

"Just about. Matilda was told what to tell you. We all know about it. We ain't exactly sorry to be seeing you go, Dunston.

It's about time, if you ask me. If it had been up to me and the Hastings boys, we'd have had you out of here long ago."

"It would have been rather difficult to get me to up and leave just by telling me to," he said.

"You should know we don't tell people to do anything, we make them do it. We could have done you and that sniveling brother of yours in at any time. You have the good Dr. Cagliostro to thank for saving your hide."

"If you'd done away with me, your young Joan of Arc wouldn't have shown up."

"Oh, her. She'll only mean trouble in the end. I told Cagliostro we'd be better off without her. I never wanted Bridget's kid here anyway."

"But she's your niece."

"She's a troublemaker, just like her mother."

Dunston saw the look in her eye and knew that it was a look of jealousy. Cagliostro would turn his daughter Julia into something more than an advocate of Satan.

"Surely she won't make trouble now that she's with her father," Dunston said, hoping to lure her into more conversation.

"Father? He ain't her father. Nobody knows who Julia's father is. Bridget was living as Cagliostro's wife, but Cagliostro didn't love her. He and I were carrying on behind Bridget's back. When Bridget found out about it, she decided to do a bit of carrying on herself. Only trouble was that she got caught by having that kid. Cagliostro intended to get rid of her anyway. He was going to marry me."

"Why didn't he?"

Rose's mouth turned down at the corners. "That's none of your damn business, Dunston."

A voice from the doorway said, "Because the good Doctor Cagliostro found himself a younger and prettier plaything. He gave Rose here the boot."

"Liar!" Rose shrieked. "He's always loved me. He still does."

Harold Hastings laughed. "Oh, sure he does, Rosy. That's

why he's all on fire for that young, pretty Julia. He'll turn himself into Adrian and she'll fall hook, line, and sinker for him."

Dunston tried to keep himself under control. Their disgusting talk was riling him, but he had to remain calm and not show his concern for Julia's welfare.

"Well," Dunston said offhandedly as he turned and went back to his car. "You can fight it all out among yourselves. I for one will be glad to get away from this rotten place and get back to where civilized people live."

"Remember, Dunston," Harold Hastings called. "Get to Peabody, collect little Danny, and get as far away from Belham as you can. If you even try to interfere, it will be the end of both of you."

Dunston slammed the door of the car and threw it into gear. He found his hands were shaking. He tightened his grip on the steering wheel. He'd be back, he swore under his breath. He'd be back and deal with every last one of them.

CHAPTER TWENTY-FIVE

The whole day had passed and Julia was afraid.

With the coming of morning came the return of her reason, and with her reason came her fears. She knew she was back in her father's house, but just where in that house, she did not know.

Wherever the room, she was a prisoner in it, and she knew why she was a prisoner. They knew now that she was fighting against them. Dunston had put her wise to their devilish practices.

She tried not to think back on the scene at the Dunston cottage, yet it kept creeping back into her mind. She remembered her father standing in the doorway in his hideous mask—if it was a mask. He had beckoned to her. She remembered the terror that had gripped her when she first set her eyes on him.

But then something strange happened. The moment his eyes fixed on hers, she found herself accepting him as a father and as a friend and had gladly walked toward him, had willingly come back to this dreadful house.

The hypnotic spell, if that's what it was, appeared to have worn off and her senses seemed back to normal. She knew the truth now and faced it squarely. Her father was indeed what Dunston had said he was. She would have to escape him or forever be damned.

Escape. But how? The door to her room was locked. She'd tried the knob at least a hundred times already. She tried it again now, rattling it so loudly the walls actually shook.

Where was Dunston? He knew she'd been taken and he could easily surmise where they'd taken her. Was he still in Peabody with Danny? No, she decided, that was yesterday. Surely he was back by this time.

Perhaps he decided to stay with his brother.

Julia felt unnerved. She wanted Dunston to worry about her, yet she knew she was being girlishly foolish in that desire. But there was something about Dunston that drew her to him. He was an intense, serious-minded, sometimes-angry young doctor, dedicated to seeking justice for his wife's unfortunate and untimely death. If he thought of her in any way at all, Julia told herself, it was as someone destined possibly for the same fate as befell his beloved Nancy.

The turning of a key in the lock swept thoughts of Dunston away and brought thoughts of possible rescue. Julia held her breath. Slowly the door creaked open. Matilda was standing there looking sinister.

"He sent me to ask what you'd like for dinner." The old cordiality was no longer in her voice. She spoke as if to a stranger, a stranger she disliked intensely.

"I'm not hungry," Julia said.

"As you wish," Matilda answered. She moved to leave. Before she could, Julia called out to her.

"Matilda. Wait."

The old woman hesitated. She turned and crossed her arms across her sagging breasts. "Well?"

"You seem so angry with me. We used to be friends, I thought."

"I'm not angry with you." Her words were icy cold.

"But I feel that you are. Why?"

"It is not you, child, with whom I am angry. It is him." She jerked her head toward the outside of the room.

"Him? My father?"

"Cagliostro is not really your father." She spat it out with vehemence. "He never showed you the certificate changing his name from Bishop to Cagliostro because there is no such document. I know I shouldn't be telling you this, but I have lost interest in living any longer with things as they are now. Cagliostro is overreaching his bounds. He is defying the Most High One. For that we will all be punished."

"Please," Julia implored. "I don't understand. You say Dr. Cagliostro is not my father?"

Matilda nodded. "That is true, but that is all I should tell you. Except that he intends making you his wife."

Julia stared at her. "His wife?"

"Cagliostro wants you. He always gets what he wants. I have tried to warn him that he is going against the wishes and dictates of the Most High One, but he scoffs at me. He thinks he is more powerful than our Lord of Darkness who gave Cagliostro all his power. He thinks he can put his powers against those of the Most High Master Satan; but he's a fool. He'll wind up destroying himself as well as the rest of us, just for the sake of his stupid love for you."

Julia knew that she had to get away from here at whatever the cost. She had to devise some plan. She could not just stand by and do nothing and expect Dunston to save her. She would have to act now, and on her own.

"You say your Master, the Most High One as you call him, had other plans for me? He does not approve of Cagliostro making me his wife?"

Matilda nodded. "Satan told us you would come in time to be sacrificed to him."

Julia turned white with fear. She thought of Dunston's young wife and the ceremonial knife. "My father, Cagliostro, is bent upon going against those instructions?"

"Yes. He plans to make you his and give you powers higher and more powerful than any of ours."

"What kind of powers?"

Matilda's eyes went wild. "Powers you never dreamed existed. Power to make yourself into anyone and anything you desire. There are no limits to the things you can do with such powers." The light suddenly went out of her eyes and she glowered angrily at Julia. "I should have been given those powers, not you. He loved me once as a young girl."

Julia looked at the old woman with surprise and disbelief. "You?"

"Oh, I am much, much younger than Cagliostro; centuries younger. He has the power to be what he chooses. I could be young and beautiful again if he would but give those powers to me, but he prefers to give them to you. You," she repeated as though it were the most disgusting word in the English language. "You, who know nothing, are nothing, came from nothing."

"But don't blame me for the situation in which I find myself. I would gladly run away if I could. I didn't ask to be brought here. I don't want to become Cagliostro's wife." A sudden thought came to her. "Matilda," she said in a low excited whisper. "Find Adrian and let him hide me somewhere until it becomes dark. Then I'll slip away. I'll never come back. You won't have to worry about my being a threat ever again."

To her surprise, Matilda laughed an evil, devilish laugh. "Adrian. Ha! There is no Adrian, only Cagliostro. I told you. He is whoever he wishes to be. He is Adrian, he is life, he is everything because the Lord of Darkness gave him that power. Because of it he thinks he is more powerful than Satan himself, as I told you. He believes he can defy the greater powers of Satan. He'll wind up destroying everything, everything!" she shrieked and turned to leave.

"No, Matilda. Wait. Why can't you help me escape? Let me run away from here before the ceremony is to take place. When is that?"

"Tomorrow night at one minute after midnight—the twenty-first anniversary of your birth."

Julia was shaking all over. "Help me escape. Once I am gone, I will no longer be a threat to any of you. I'll go far, far away...." She didn't finish because Matilda was shaking her head from side to side.

"No, you can never go away."

"But I must, for all our sakes."

"There is only one way you can help us and yourself."

"Tell me and I'll do it," Julia said anxiously.

The old woman gazed deeply into her eyes. She narrowed her lids until they were tiny slits. "Let us sacrifice you."

Old Matilda laughed and started to leave again.

"Wait," Julia called.

Again the old woman turned back and patiently waited for Julia to say what she intended saying.

"Can this sacrifice be done without Cagliostro's knowledge?"

"There is that possibility. I do not have his unlimited powers, but I do have certain powers equal to his. It is possible that we might sacrifice you without his knowing of it."

"How could this be accomplished?"

Matilda screwed up her face and began to plot. "Well," she said slowly. "There is a sacrificial altar in the cellar of the inn which could be used for the rites. I'll hide you someplace else in the house until the time comes for the sacrifice. I can tell Cagliostro that you've been spirited away by that Dunston man. Knowing Cagliostro, he'll fly off in search of Dunston, and we will be free to do what the Lord of Darkness has decreed be done with you."

Julia only half listened as the old woman spoke her mind aloud. She knew she must be looking deathly white and that she was noticeably shaking from head to foot. But all she could think about was finding some way out of this room, out of this house. It would be easier to escape from a feeble old woman than from Cagliostro, who was a tower of virility.

"Then do it," she said evenly. "I would be willing to be sacrificed rather than live as the wife of that monster."

Old Matilda gave her a suspicious eye. She saw the determined look on Julia's face. She knew that Julia would try to trick her somehow, but Matilda told herself she could easily watch out for any of the young girl's devious little tricks. She'd handle the silly young girl. She was powerful, almost as powerful as the great Cagliostro. She would sacrifice the girl, and Satan would reward her with powers far beyond any Cagliostro could conceive.

Keeping a wary eye on Julia, Matilda pushed the door outward, opening it all the way. She stepped aside. "Come with me then," Matilda said. "We'll hide you in another part of the house."

Julia acted without thinking, without knowing exactly what she was doing. The minute she stepped into the corridor, she grabbed the edge of the door and flung it backward. It struck Matilda just as she had planned for it to do. Hastily she turned the key and dashed along the corridor, running blindly to whatever fate held in store for her.

CHAPTER TWENTY-SIX

The house was silent as a tomb.

Julia went quickly along the dark corridor trying to find some way out. She was in a part of the cellar, she thought, noticing the small windows far above her head. The windows were too high up to reach, and too small to climb through even if she were able to reach one of them.

She made a turn in the corridor and, to her surprise, she saw something that looked familiar—crates and boxes and barrels, stacks of straw and piles of sawdust, a statue without its head and the one with a broken arm. She was in her father's store-room.

Her father? The word sounded odious to her. She could never think of that man again as her father. The very mention of the word "father" made her stomach queasy. How could she have been so blind as to let herself be so easily taken in? But she had wanted parents at whatever the cost. She knew now that the cost was much too high to pay.

She mustn't think of anything now but escape. Everything else was secondary to getting out of this house. She would worry about Cagliostro and the others once she was safely away from here.

She looked around, trying to get her bearings. She said a silent prayer for guidance and deliverance. and wandered into the maze of boxes and crates, bales and packages that cluttered up the place. As if in answer to her prayer, a stairway appeared directly in front of her. She recognized it—or thought she did—

as the same stairway she'd mounted once before—the stairway that led her outside the house.

Without a moment's hesitation she went up. She inched open the door at the top of the landing and peered out. She saw the wide lawn, the bushes, the trees, the edge of the woods. Her heart stopped for a second when she saw something else, something she had never expected to see again. He was standing in the shadow of a tree, but his fair hair glinted in the fading light of the sun, glinted just long enough to catch Julia's eye.

"Dunston," she said softly. Her pulse beat faster, the blood rushed more wildly through her veins. She eased the door open wide enough to slip through. The moment she showed herself, Dunston emerged from his hiding place. He raised his arm and motioned for her to come ahead. She ran as if the Devil himself were after her. A moment later she collapsed into Dunston's arms. He pulled her into the shadow of the trees.

"Oh, Dunston," she sobbed as her fears brought forth her tears.

"I don't know how you ever got out of there, Julia, but that will have to wait. As much as I enjoy holding you like this, we'd better get the blazes out of here, and fast."

She gave a frightened look toward the house. "I locked Matilda in the cellar. Cagliostro is in the house somewhere. Do you think he saw me running across the lawn?"

"We can't take that chance. Come on." He grabbed her hand. He wished he could enfold her, embrace her, calm her fears, kiss away her tears. She was safe. He was with her again. Danny was safe. They had a life ahead of them after all. It hadn't ended as he feared it might.

"Where are we going?" Julia managed to ask as they ran blindly through the forest.

"I think the old, abandoned church is our best bet. We'll hide under the stained-glass window. They'll be afraid to come looking for us there and if they do, the cross will protect us."

Swearing silently under his breath, he admonished himself for not having thought to bring some relics or talismans to protect them. He'd given everything to Danny to insure his safety, not realizing that he was leaving Julia and himself vulnerable, naked of any holy article. The stained-glass window was their only sanctuary.

They skirted the town, taking the route that was heavily wooded. By the time they reached the old, abandoned church, the sky was pitch black. Not even a moon hung suspended in it.

They went in through the rear door and hurried toward the altar niche. Strangely enough, Julia did not feel the same fears she'd experienced when first she saw the niche with its cross-shaped stained-glass window. Now, in fact, the cross was comforting and peaceful. It seemed to be stretching out its arms to welcome and embrace and protect her. She smiled up at the window.

"I hadn't noticed how beautiful it is," she said softly.

"Come," Dunston said as he took her hand and pulled her behind the altar where they settled themselves directly beneath the stained-glass cross. Julia sighed and leaned her head on his shoulder. Her body ached. She felt suddenly more tired than she'd ever felt in her life.

Still, she was with Dunston and she felt totally at peace. She pressed her head harder against his shoulder and felt his arms go around her. He laid his cheek against her hair and they sat silent and still, letting the quiet tranquility of the old church settle about them.

"Danny?" Julia asked after a while. "Is he all right?"

"He's still in his trance." He proceeded to tell her about his meeting up with Matilda and the choice she'd offered him. "I went to Peabody and put Danny back inside a pentacle. The hospital staff was convinced I was off my rocker, but I told them that it was part of our religious beliefs. Hospitals never interfere with a patient's religious beliefs, so they let me do what I wanted. Don't worry about Danny. He's safe and sound. Nothing can harm him now."

"Then shouldn't we be away from here?"

"We must wait here until after your twenty-first birthday.

Once that is past you will be safe. I studied a lot about Satanism and I know that their sacrifices must never be performed on anyone over the age of twenty-one. You are something special to them, I believe. They mean more for you than just a simple sacrifice."

"Cagliostro means to take me as his wife," Julia told him.

"Then they told you that Cagliostro is not really your father?"

"Matilda told me." She thought for a moment. "Why did he pretend he was?"

"From what I can gather, I believe he's had tabs on you ever since Bridget Bishop's baby was taken away from her. I believe it was all Cagliostro's doing right from the very start. Your Aunt Rose told me that her sister, Bridget—your mother—lived with Cagliostro as his wife, but Cagliostro loved Rose and not Bridget. Bridget found out about it and got jealous, and in order to get even, she started to carry on with some other man. Rose never said who. You were the offspring of that romance."

Julia felt a sinking feeling in the pit of her stomach.

"I'm sorry, Julia. It isn't a very pretty picture. But at least you are not Cagliostro's daughter, although he tried every trick he knew to make everyone believe you were."

Julia thought of the gypsy, the medium, the face in the crystal ball, of Adrian, the séance, the luck and ease with which she'd found her birth record at the orphanage. Cagliostro had been following her, preparing her path, leading her to Belham. She had always sensed the presence of evil following her wherever she went. She knew now that it had been Cagliostro who hovered at her back.

Dunston let out a deep breath. "It's difficult to believe that there are such fiends as Cagliostro in the world. To think that that man arranged for the death of your mother and then had you spirited away to an orphanage until you were ripe to marry according to his devilish doctrines. What a monster he is."

Julia remembered and orange face, the yellow eyes, the fire-colored hair. "Monster indeed," she said softly. "But Matilda tells me he can change himself at will. According to her, he really is the infamous Count Cagliostro, to whom Satan gave eternal life and strong powers."

"Eternal life?"

"Yes. Matilda said his powers are limitless and that he is centuries old."

"Then he is incapable of being destroyed."

Julia sighed and gazed into the darkness of the church. "Can evil ever be completely wiped out? It will always be with us, Dunston. Nothing can remove it from the face of the earth."

"But I must try, Julia. I must try," Dunston said, gritting his teeth and clenching his fists. "Cagliostro must be destroyed."

"You know that it's useless. We are powerless against him. Surely you realize that."

"But there must be a way."

Julia suddenly sat up. "Wait," she said. "Perhaps there is a way. Matilda said—"

Just then someone outside called Julia's name. Dunston jumped up and peeked through a broken corner of the window. He saw a cluster of townspeople with torches. They began chanting: "Julia, Julia, Julia...."

"They know we're in here," Dunston said. "Don't be afraid. I don't think they'll dare enter the church. All we need do is sit tight and wait it out. If we don't go outside, we will be safe enough from them."

"Oh, Dunston, I'm so frightened. They'll set fire to the church. They'll burn us alive."

Dunston held her. "No, I don't think we have to worry about that. Cagliostro wants you alive, not dead."

"But the others want me sacrificed. Matilda...all of them...."

"Sacrificed, yes, but not murdered. Besides, the ceremony must take place at the very second of your twenty-first birthday." He shook his head. "No, I don't think they'll do anything but try to lure us out of the church."

Again Julia hugged him. "I'm afraid, Dunston," she sobbed.

"Don't be, Julia. I'm with you now. I'll protect you. They can't hurt you anymore. Try to ignore their chanting and get some sleep. I promise you we'll be safe here. They can't get to us as long as we are under the protection of the crucifix."

Julia shivered and cuddled closer to Dunston. The night was just beginning. The hours would be long and each of them would be filled with danger. The chanting went on and on.

She was not aware that she slept until she heard the crow of the cock and felt the warm stray beams of sunlight play on her cheek. She stirred, reluctant to open her eyes.

She felt Dunston move. He cleared his throat and shook his head slightly. "I didn't think I'd fall asleep but I did," he confessed.

"I did too," she told him.

He smiled down at her. "I know." He glanced toward the broken corner of the window. "They stopped their chanting just before dawn. Thoughtful of the little beggars to give us a couple of hours sleep at least."

Julia eased herself away from him and stretched. She felt the ache in her muscles and found that Dunston had put his jacket around her shoulders. When she tried to stand, she gave a little groan of pain as her legs threatened to buckle under her. "Oh, I'm cramped," she complained.

"And hungry, I'll bet," he said.

She found herself smiling, something she never thought she'd be capable of again. "Ravenous," she admitted.

"Well, I wish I could supply the bacon and eggs, but I'm afraid we'll have to wait until tomorrow morning for that. Do you think you can hold out until then?"

"Do I have a choice?" Julia asked, returning the flippancy.

He laughed softly, liking her spirit. In fact, as he gazed at her, he suddenly realized he liked just about everything about her.

"Do you think it would be all right if we opened the back door and got some fresh air into this place?" Julia asked.

"We could open it a crack. I see no harm in that." He went over and pulled the door open a half foot or so. "It sure is a beautiful day...." Suddenly his voice trailed off and Julia saw his eyes widen as he stared out into the sunlight.

Julia pulled the door open wide and looked out. There, emerging from the woods at the back of the church, was Dunston's younger brother.

"Danny," Julia breathed.

They watched, opened mouthed, as the boy came swiftly toward them. Suddenly a wild beast appeared behind him at the edge of the wood. The beast growled, showing its sharp, gleaming teeth. Danny heard the growl and turned. He froze in horror for a moment, then he pivoted and started to run, not toward the church, but toward the town.

"No, Danny," Dunston yelled. He threw himself out of the door and raced as fast as he could toward his brother. The hairy beast was gaining on the young boy. Danny veered sharply and dashed into the woods, the animal close on his heels.

"Danny." Dunston too disappeared into the woods.

Julia stood in the doorway for what seemed an eternity, praying softly for the safety of Dunston and Danny.

Her prayers were violently interrupted by a loud shattering, splintering noise at her back. She whirled around just in time to see a fissure eat its way up from the corner to the very top of the stained-glass window. She screamed as the glass came pouring down and crumbled into a million tiny fragments.

A man appeared in the opening where the window had been. He was tall, dressed all in black, his face the color of the setting sun, his eyes flashing yellow.

"It is time, my pretty," he snarled. "You'll not escape me this time."

CHAPTER TWENTY-SEVEN

Dunston ran blindly into the tree-choked forest. The brush made him stumble more than once and branches scratched his skin. "Danny, Danny!" he yelled, but he saw neither his brother running nor the pursuing beast.

He suddenly heard a fiendish laugh. The laugh faded in the distance, but he heard a woman scream. He knew in an instant it was Julia.

Suddenly, a young boy appeared from the mist, walking slowly, silently toward Dunston. "Danny." Dunston sighed with relief and went toward his brother. But as he got closer, the boy began to dissolve into the mist.

Dunston cursed himself, knowing now that it had all been a trick. Cagliostro had duped him into thinking he saw Danny being pursued by a vicious animal. But it wasn't Danny at all; it had only been a vision. He swore at himself for having been so easily fooled.

The echo of Julia's scream sounded in his ears. Cagliostro's trick had worked. He had managed neatly to get Dunston away and then somehow had lured Julia out from under the protection of the crucifix. He again had her in his power.

He tightened his hands into fists. She would not remain in his power for very long, he swore. If it meant his life, he would save Julia from the terrible fate Cagliostro had in store for her. But how?

* * * * * * *

The hours ticked away. The bright summer day turned dark, as a warm night settled down over the town. Dunston was frantic. He could come up with no solution to the problem. He'd worked his way secretly to Cagliostro's house, but he could find no way in. The door through which Julia had escaped was locked from the outside. The only other means of access to the house was through the front or rear doors, both of which would easily expose his presence. Dunston was well aware that they were on the lookout for him. He knew too he would have to be very careful if he intended to get Julia to safety.

He heard the town clock toll eleven. He had only an hour before it would be over and Julia would be lost to him forever.

Only an hour, he reminded himself. He crouched behind the bushes at the edge of the woods and tried desperately to think of some way to gain entry to Cagliostro's house. Yet, even if he did get inside, how would he know where to look for Julia? Their sacrificial room was obviously hidden somewhere. She'd mentioned a secret room, but she hadn't told him where it was or how to gain access to it. He glanced at his watch and saw that four more minutes had slipped by.

Suddenly he heard the sound of a horse's hoofbeats. Dunston crouched behind the bushes and peered down the road. A magnificent white stallion was approaching, ridden by a young, handsome man. Behind them was a procession of people all dressed in long black robes, belted at the middle and hooded at the top.

As he waited for them to pass, he carefully broke off two straight sticks from the bush that hid him and used his shoe lace to create a crude crucifix from the two sticks. He closed his eyes, said a silent prayer and kissed the little wooden cross.

"...and deliver us from evil. Amen."

He stayed hidden until the people filed by. As the last robed figure went by him, Dunston scurried from behind the bush and spaced himself just behind the final man. He timed his step with the others and kept an even distance between them. He waited until they were in the last clump of trees before he made his move.

Quickly he reached in front of him and tightened his fingers at the back of the man's neck. He squeezed his thumb into the vein, cutting off the flow of blood to the brain. He applied a quick, steady pressure. Almost instantly the figure collapsed without a sound.

Dunston scooped him up in his arms and deposited him behind a clump of shrubs, stripped the robe from the body and donned it himself. He kicked off his shoes and ran without making a sound until he caught up with the chanting line of townspeople. No one turned to look at him; no one had known what had taken place. Dunston pulled the hood well over his head, tucking his face into its recess, and followed doggedly along behind the procession as it neared Cagliostro's house.

They went around to the side of the house. Magically, a trellis moved aside, exposing a doorway. The horse and rider disappeared down a ramp. The robed figures followed. Dunston found himself going down into what was obviously the cellar. The slope was steep and cold and damp.

They came into a large square room lighted by candles. Strange tracings covered the walls. In the center of the room was a huge, gold figure of Satan, complete with horns, tail, and claws. One by one the figures knelt and kissed the cloven hooves of the figure. Dunston was the last to kneel and after he had kissed the figure's feet, he saw the horse being led into another room. The rider returned a moment later and began to chant. The others huddled together and picked up the chant.

Dunston sneaked a look at his watch. It was eleven thirty-five.

The chanting went on for several minutes. Then the rider threw up his hands and invoked the powers of hell. The golden statue was suddenly obscured by billowing smoke and tongues of fire that shot up all around it. It sank mysteriously into the floor. As it disappeared out of sight a wall slid away, exposing a staircase that led up. Again the procession regrouped in single file and went slowly up the stairs, chanting softly to themselves.

They entered a circular room, draped all in black with black-marble flooring. The room was ablaze with light from hundreds of candles. Dunston gasped when he looked toward the raised platform on which an altar had been erected. Julia knelt before it, struggling with Cagliostro and Matilda.

Julia's hands were tied behind her back with silken cords. She wore a pure-white robe with blood-red trim. Her feet were bare, her hair fell straight and loose from her bowed head. Dunston used every ounce of willpower he had to restrain himself from rushing to her and gathering her into his arms.

"Regie Satanas!" Cagliostro called.

"Regie Satanas!" the gathered flock echoed.

"Ave Satanas!"

"Ave Satanas!"

"Satan rules the Earth!"

"Satan rules the Earth!"

Dunston kept his eyes fixed steadily on Julia. She did not raise her head. She struggled with her ropes and Matilda kept her hand on Julia's shoulder, trying to keep her still.

Cagliostro lifted a long, pointed sword from the top of the black-marble altar. Moving it clockwise, he pointed to the north, east, south, and west. He stopped at each cardinal point of the compass saying: "O Mighty Prince of Hell. Leviathan from the north, Satan from the east, Belial from the south, Lucifer from the west. We call unto you, O High and Noble Lord of Darkness. We are here and we await your coming."

A wild wind suddenly blew through the room, fluttering the flames of the candles, extinguishing some of them. The room began to vibrate. Suddenly a voice boomed out: "You will not disobey," the voice thundered.

All of the robed figures cowered and gasped with fear. Before the altar, Cagliostro straightened himself and looked defiant. Matilda's eyes moved nervously in their sockets.

"We are equal now, O Great One," Cagliostro said.

There was a hideous laugh that chilled the marrow of the bones.

Cagliostro continued to look undaunted. "Show yourself, Prince of Hell, and we will converse as equals. This girl is to be my wife. I will not sacrifice her."

"You will do as I directed," the voice boomed.

"I cannot," Cagliostro called, braving the terrible voice that thundered throughout the room.

"Sacrifice!" the mysterious voice boomed.

The robed figures suddenly took up the word. "Sacrifice, sacrifice...," they chanted.

Cagliostro raised the sword, signaling for quiet. Again a gust of wind blasted through the room. The sword in Cagliostro's hand was suddenly flipped into the air. It hung suspended as everyone stared up at it. Then slowly it began moving toward Cagliostro's breast.

"Sacrifice," the voice said. "Sacrifice or I shall thrust this blade through your body. Only I can take away your eternal life." The sword drew closer and closer.

Cagliostro suddenly cowered and fell to his knees as though giant hands had pressed him into subservience.

"I demand that the girl be sacrificed to me," the voice demanded.

"Sacrifice! Sacrifice!" the crowd yelled.

Cagliostro's shoulders slumped. He looked longingly at Julia's bowed head. "Sacrifice," he murmured, nodding his head.

Matilda hooted and began jigging about. She ripped off her robe and exposed her withered naked body for all to see. The other celebrants kept chanting, "Sacrifice, sacrifice, sacrifice...." One by one they stripped naked and began cavorting before the altar.

Dunston knew he must act now or all would be lost. He pulled the small wooden crucifix from his inside pocket and leaped up on the platform next to Cagliostro. He held up the cross. The sword that was hovering in air clattered to the floor immediately. For a moment the gathering froze in shock. Then, recognizing Dunston when he threw off his robe, they crouched and started toward him looking not unlike a pack of starving wolves threatening to devour their prey.

"Stand back," Dunston yelled, holding up the cross.

Julia raised her head. "Dunston," she cried through her tears.

Cagliostro was still kneeling before the altar. He had been too taken by surprise to move. But now that the shock had worn off, he got to his feet and advanced toward Dunston.

"Stay where you are," Dunston ordered, holding the cross in front of him and avoiding Cagliostro's eyes. Dunston reached down and helped Julia to her feet. He managed to untie the cords that bound her wrists while keeping the others at bay.

He did not see Cagliostro's long, thick fingers encircle the base of a candlestick and lift it slightly. Dunston only saw the flaming candle as it was thrown at him. He ducked just in time. The candle rolled from its holder and flew against the wall. Its flames began to lick at the black, heavy draperies.

Dunston was careful not to lose the cross. He held it before him like a shield and, holding tight to Julia, he backed away from the altar, his eyes flicking to the right and left, looking for some way out.

Julia remembered the panel that was guarded by Anubis and guided him back toward where she thought it was. But when she looked back toward the exit, she saw nothing but draperies covering every inch of the walls. At one side of the altar the flames were reaching upward. Everyone else was too absorbed with the wooden cross to pay any attention to the flames. They all stood transfixed before the holy symbol.

When Dunston and Julia reached the draperies, they found that they covered an empty and open doorway. Quickly they ducked through it. Dunston placed the crucifix on the floor to guard and protect their escape. They found themselves in the parlor.

There was a bursting noise at their backs as the fire broke out and engulfed the room. In their flight, Julia bumped the arm of Anubis without being aware of it and the paneling slid closed, locking Cagliostro and the others inside the secret room. They heard the yells and the screams, but did not realize that there was no way for the Devil worshippers to get out of the secret room.

A loud explosion followed and the whole house shook. Fire was shooting all around them.

"This way," Julia yelled, grabbing Dunston's hand and pulling him out into the foyer. The front doors were securely locked and there was no key in the lock. Dunston didn't hesitate. He smashed the glass door panel. The draft of air that rushed into the house sucked the fire toward them.

Dunston struggled with the door. Finding himself unable to open it, he put his shoulder to the frame and broke it down. The fire was through the parlor and started to creep up the horse-shoe-shaped staircase.

Julia turned and glanced for the last time on the home that she had thought was where she belonged. The brief happiness she had found there was going up in smoke and she was glad to see it go.

Dunston pulled her outside just as the flames shot through the windows, smashing them out, spewing glass fragments out onto the porch. Like a house of cardboard, the place became a torch. Flames were everywhere they looked.

They ran across the lawn, then stopped and looked back at the blazing inferno.

He wrapped his arms around her as the house crackled and burned and began to break up

"It's finished," he said simply.

ABOUT THE AUTHOR

V. J. BANIS is the critically acclaimed author ("the master's touch in storytelling..."—*Publishers Weekly*) of more than 200 published books and numerous short stories in a career spanning nearly a half century. A native of Ohio and a longtime Californian, he lives and writes now in West Virginia's beautiful Blue Ridge.

You can visit him at http://www.vjbanis.com